THE COINCIDENCE MYSTERIES: THE EVERMORE

(THE COINCIDENCE MYSTERIES, #1)

JESSICA SORENSEN

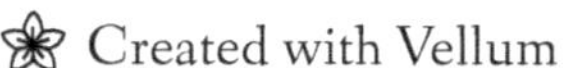

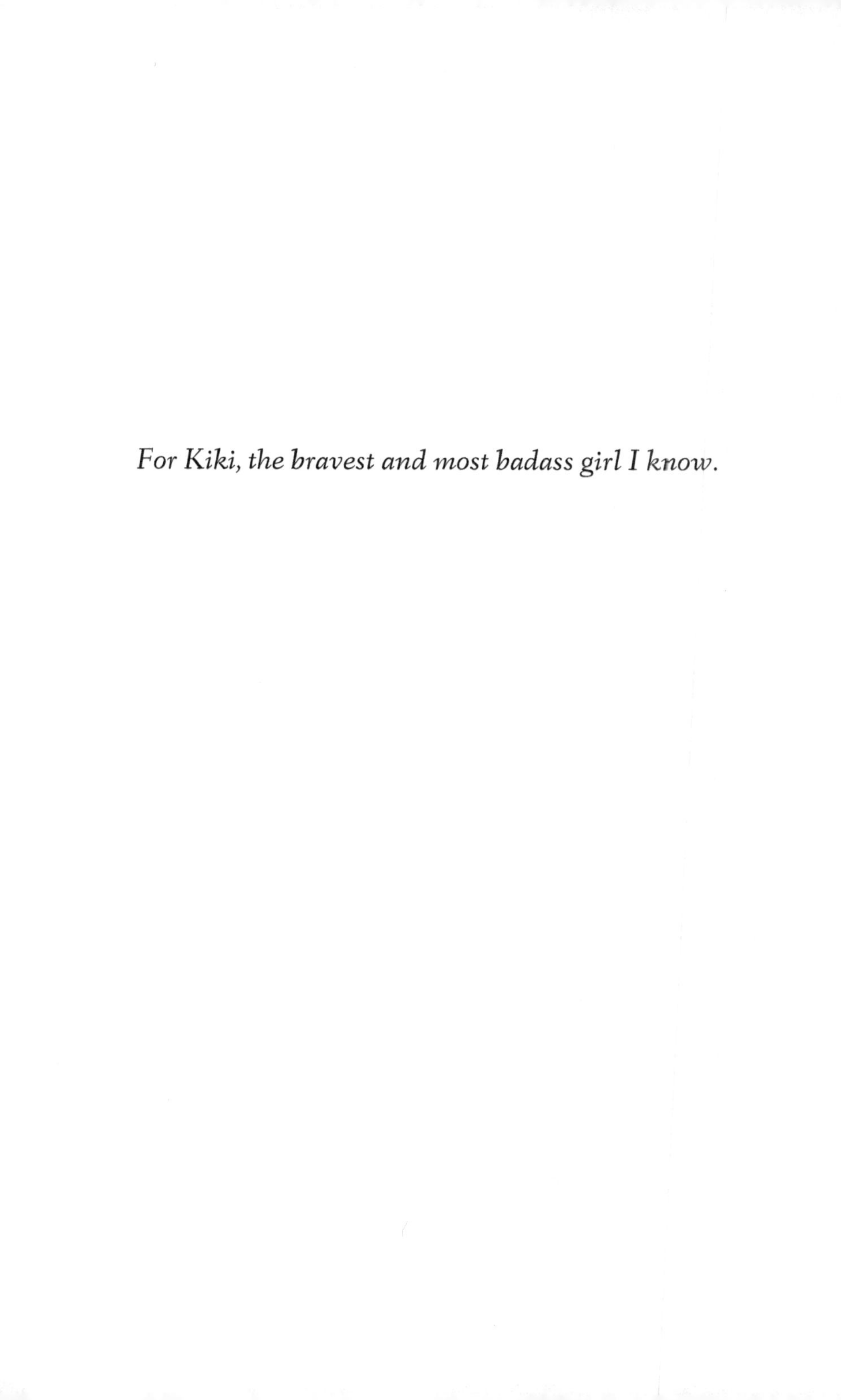

For Kiki, the bravest and most badass girl I know.

ONE
CALLIE

MY HEART IS RACING, my adrenaline is soaring, and my palms are disgustingly sticky. I'm nervous. More nervous than I've been in a really long time.

"You doing okay?" the secretary sitting behind the desk asks while eyeballing my bouncing knee.

I nod and try to hold still. "Yeah, I'm great." I wipe my sweaty palms on the sides of my jeans, feeling ridiculous. *Why am I so nervous? It's just a job interview. You've done this before, Callie.*

But you want this job really badly.

I internally sigh. *I need to calm down, or I'm going to mess up the interview.*

The secretary offers me a sympathetic smile. "Evie should be here soon. Just try to hang in there a little longer, okay?" He winks at me then redirects his attention to the computer on his desk.

I'm not sure what to make of his wink, since secretaries usually don't wink at potential new employees. Then again, nothing about this place resembles a typical business office.

Take the secretary. He looks maybe a few years older than me with messy blond hair and a couple of piercings in his lips and brow. He's wearing a shirt with a skull on it and an array of leather bands ornament his wrists. And when he got up to get something from the printer earlier, I noticed he didn't have on any shoes.

When I first walked into the office and saw him sitting behind the desk, frantically digging through the desk drawer, I thought maybe he had snuck in and was about to steal something. But then he greeted me with a friendly smile and asked me if I had an appointment. That's when I realized I judged him simply on his looks and felt terrible about it. That's also when I realized just how strange this office is.

That revelation sent a bit of relief through me. I had decided to quit my last job of writing articles for an online website because it was boring and kind of repetitious. I've always loved writing, but that job sucked the enjoyment out of it. Still, it was a job and paid decently. But a few after I first started, and rounding into the end of my sophomore year, I craved a change. I wanted to be able to wake up in the morning and be pumped to go to work. And yeah, I realize a lot of people don't love their jobs. But, for me, writing sometimes feels like creating art. And forcing art usually doesn't work very well. And in my case, it didn't. Sure, the articles I wrote were decent enough, but not great. And I wanted—want—to do something great.

I just needed to figure out what that was.

So, after running the idea of changing jobs by Kayden —which of course, he supported—I made a choice to start applying for jobs that sounded appealing. A handful of applications and callbacks later, and here I am, at the untraditional *The Offbeat Go Daily*, waiting for an interview.

I'm not going to lie, the name of the place was what drew me in. Usually, I'm more of a traditional sort of person, but the name screams adventurous and I've been wanting that lately. Then I started reading some of their published articles and columns and wow, just wow, I really want to write for them. Not only do they cover tough, unconventional topics, but their writers are extremely detailed, as if they experienced the event first-hand. It sounded like the complete opposite of my old job, which preferred that I list only the basic facts and never write pieces that would offend people, even though that isn't possible—someone will always be offended no matter how careful I am with my words.

"You want a sucker?" The secretary interrupts my thoughts.

I blink up from the floor and find him leaning over his desk with a huge jar of suckers in his hand.

Definitely the first time I've been offered a sucker at a job interview.

"Um, sure." I push to my feet, dig out a pink one, and peel off the wrapper. "Thanks." I pop the sucker into my mouth and grind my teeth against it, trying to alleviate my stress.

"Suckers are awesome stress relievers, right?" He sets the jar down on the cluttered desk.

I nod, removing the sucker from my mouth. "Is it that obvious how nervous I am?" I bite down on my tongue. It might not be the smartest move to tell the secretary of the place you're hoping to get hired at that you're nervous.

He shrugs, leaning back in his chair and popping a sucker into his mouth. "All the potential newbies usually are, so don't sweat it." He swivels the chair from side to side, the sucker clanking against his teeth. "A little advice. Evie's pretty chill. She'll probably ask you a few questions about your past jobs and your experience. But mostly, she'll just ask you about your life and then come to a decision on whether or not she likes you."

"But how will she know if I'm a good writer then?"

"She's already read some of your work. If she hadn't, you wouldn't be here."

"Oh." My palms begin to sweat again as my nervousness begins to grow.

He smiles. "That's a good thing, Callie. It means she likes your work."

"Right." I nod, pretending I'm more relaxed than I am. Really, I'm a nervous wreck.

This place is so different from what I'm used to, but I guess that's what I'm looking for, right?

I sure hope so.

You'll be fine, Callie. You can do this. You have the qualifications, you've done your research, and you wore your lucky outfit.

My lucky outfit consists of a black button top, pinstriped pants, and black heels with white stripes over the toes. It's the same outfit I wore when I got my first job and the one after that.

Of course, my confidence flies right out the window when a woman rushes into the office, wearing holey jeans, a black T-shirt, a studded belt, and a pair of clunky boots. She looks as though she was just at a concert and at first I wonder if she's a journalist here, but then the secretary calls her Evie.

That's Evie?

I think I may have overdressed…

No, you're fine. You look professional and tidy.

I mentally shake my head at myself. *Take a look around you, Callie. This place isn't looking for professional and tidy.*

The secretary grins at Evie as she stops in front of the desk, red-faced and out of breath. "You're late."

She tosses her bag into the open door to an office then combs her fingers through her purple and black hair. "I know. I know. But my car wouldn't start, and then I got an email from…" Her gaze lands on me. "You don't work for me, do you?"

I shift in my seat. "Um, no. I'm Callie Lawrence. I'm here for the job interview."

"It's your three o'clock," the secretary adds, reaching for a coffee mug.

She glances at him and he raises his brows with an amused twinkle in his eyes.

"Oh, yeah, right. My three o'clock." She eyeballs me over. From the unimpressed look in her eyes, I'm betting my lucky outfit is going to be no longer lucky. "Well, why don't you come into my office so we can get this started."

Nodding, I rise to my feet and follow her inside the office that consists of a cluttered desk, a computer, and a window with a view of the parking lot. A typical office except for the hundreds of newspaper clippings, articles, and photos taped to the walls.

"It's how I keep my research organized," she clarifies when she notes me staring at her walls. "I know it looks pretty chaotic, but I swear there's a system to it. Well, if you can call chaos a system." The corners of her lips quirk as she plops down into a chair.

The trace of a smile gives me a drop of hope that perhaps I haven't completely failed the interview yet.

"Go ahead, have a seat." She gestures at a chair in front of me. "And tell me a little bit about yourself and why you want to work here."

I toss the sucker into a trashcan then sink down into the chair and discreetly wipe my damp palms on my legs for the tenth time. "My name's Callie Lawrence, which you already know. I'm a sophomore at UW and majoring in English—"

She holds up her hand, cutting me off, and my nerves skyrocket.

"I know your credentials—I read the resume you sent in. I'm not looking to hear a repeat of it. What I want to know is what makes you unique in the sea of journalists out there. Because *The Offbeat Go Daily* is all about unique. We pride ourselves on interesting stories no one else is reporting and different angles. A lot of our projects require our journalists to do a bit of undercover work, and some of the jobs can be sketchy sometimes and require a lot of thinking outside the box. But I can't figure out if you're the type of person who fits that profile just based upon a resume." She rests her arms on her desk. "So tell me a little bit about yourself that I didn't already read about on your resume—tell me your life story, the good and the bad." She slants forward. "Tell me how you became the Callie Lawrence that's sitting in front of me today."

Seriously?

I resist the urge to bite my fingernails, even though I desperately want to. "Um, well, where do I start?"

"How about from the beginning?" she suggests, reclining back in her chair. "And don't leave out the easy or difficult parts. It's those that are going to make you stand out."

So, she wants to know my story. Like my life story. The good and the bad. Do I have the guts to do it? Tell her all the important facts that made me who I am today. About how the last year or so, I've lived a pretty ordinary, but lovely life. How on my twelfth birthday my brother's best friend stole my good life away and shattered me when he raped me. How I locked the secret up and it ate away at me on the inside, nearly destroying me. How I lost all my friends. Was called a freak. Was bullied. How I slinked in the shadows, wishing I was invisible until the day I coincidently crossed paths with Kayden Owens while his dad was beating him. How that night would change my life forever in the best way possible. How when I went to college, I started to heal. How I fell in love. How I finally told my secret.

How I became Callie Lawrence who dreams of writing articles and pieces that will help others who are stuck in the darkness.

I take a deep breath. "Well, I was born in..."

TWO
KAYDEN

"HEY, man, are you coming to the party tonight?" Jason, a guy who plays on the field with me, asks as we head out of the classroom.

"I'm not sure yet." Honestly, I probably won't. While I've never minded a party here or there, I'm starting to grow tired of them. Plus, Callie's not a huge fan. And between jobs, school, and practices, we don't have a lot of free time, so every ounce of free time we get, we try to spend it together. "Probably not."

He rolls his eyes. "You never come, man. What's up with that?"

I shrug as I dig my phone from out of my pocket as it buzzes. "I'm just not that in to parties."

He walks with me as I make a right down the crowded

hallway, heading for the exit doors. "You sure that's all it is?"

"Yeah. What else would it be about?"

"I don't know. Maybe something else."

I just start to read the incoming message, which is from Seth, but the insinuation in his tone causes me to glance up at him. "If you want to say something, just spit it out."

Jason has never been my favorite person. He's cocky and kind of a snob, which causes friction on the field. Normally, I don't hang out with people like him, but there's this sort of unwritten rule that even off the field, the team has to act decently to each other.

He shrugs, stuffing his hands into his pockets. "Some of the guys and I are wondering if you don't come to the team's parties because that uptight girlfriend of yours won't let you."

At first I don't think I heard him right, mostly because Callie has never come off as uptight to anyone. Shy and quiet, sure. But uptight?

"Are you fucking kidding me right now?" I slow to a stop and step toward him.

He's a couple of inches shorter than me but has got me by at least fifty pounds. Still, my height gives off the intimidation factor I need, and he steps back an inch or two.

"Look, I didn't mean anything by it." He raises his hands in front of him.

"Didn't mean anything by it?" I crook my brow at him. "You called my girlfriend uptight, which she's not. And you've met her like what? A total of two times, so how the hell would you know what kind of a person she is?"

"Sorry man." He looks anything but sorry. "Maybe uptight was the wrong choice of words."

"Maybe you shouldn't be talking about my girlfriend at all."

"Maybe not." He backs away with a trace of a smirk on his face. What the smirk means is beyond me, but it raises my anger to a whole new level.

Shaking my head, I storm down the hallway in the opposite direction of Jason. When I reach the doors at the end, I push outside and step beneath the cloudy sky. The cool autumn breeze sweeps over me as I stride across the grass toward my car so I can drive over to the practice stadium where I'll spend the entire evening working out and running plays with the team. Then I'll go home and hang with Callie for about an hour until I pass out. Early morning, five days a week, I go to work, afternoons are reserved for classes, and weekends are for games.

My routine is pretty hardcore right now, but I'm preparing for my future. But I miss Callie a lot. Even though we live with each other, I barely see her. Right now she's in between jobs, so we do have a bit of extra time. But a couple of weeks ago when she was working, I didn't even get that hour at night. The only thing that helps me continue with this stressful schedule is that eventually, I'll make it to a point where my entire life won't be a crazy mess of rushing here and there. Then I'll be able to take care of Callie like she does me and then I'll get to spend more time with her.

As I reach my car, my phone buzzes again, reminding me I never read the message from Seth. This text is from him too. Knowing Seth, he more than likely sent me some silly meme—yeah, he's that friend. So when I open the text and see that it's an actual message, I grow worried. Especially when I see it has to do with Callie.

Seth: Any chance you can skip out on practice? Our darling little Callie is upset and could use some cuddle time, and unfortunately, my cuddles don't seem to cheer her up much. Don't know why. I've been told I'm like the best cuddler ever.

My worry immediately magnifies as I hurry and climb in my car.

Me: Is everything okay?

Seth: Yeah, it's not like an emergency. I

think she's just bummed out about the job interview, and you two have barely seen each other for the last couple of weeks, so I think some Kayden cuddle time might cheer her up. She won't ask you herself. You know how she is about asking you to do things for her, especially stuff like skip out on practices.

I start up my car.

Me: Yeah, I know. She's always putting everyone else before herself.

I really do know that. And it's part of the reason why I got so pissed off about Jason calling her uptight. Sure, Callie isn't a flirt that giggles twenty-four seven like most of the girls Jason hangs out with. No, Callie isn't like that at all. She's one of the sweetest, most unselfish, caring people I know. She's perfect, even when she's having a bad day, even when we're pissed off at each other.

Perfection. That's what Callie is.

Seth: So, are you coming then?

While practice is important, I haven't missed one in forever. And cheering Callie up seems more important at the moment. After all, she's always there to cheer me up.

Me: Yep, on my way.

After I text my coach that I'm not feeling well and I'm going to have to take the night off, I drop the phone into the cup holder, strap my seat belt on, and press on the gas to maneuver out of the parking space. As I'm steering the car toward the road, something strange catches my attention. A guy in his mid-twenties, wearing a button-down shirt, a pair of jeans, and a baseball cap is standing by a black SUV with extremely tinted windows. He has a strange look on his face as his gaze tracks my car. I don't know what he's looking at, since the vehicle I drive is nothing spectacular. What really creeps me out, though, is that the moment my car passes him, he climbs into his SUV and backs out of the parking space. Then he pulls out onto the road behind me and follows me for a handful of blocks. Starting to get a bit uneasy, I take a detour into a random subdivision, figuring I'm just being paranoid. But he still follows me.

"Shit. Who the hell could this dude be?" I continue to drive around the streets that weave through the two-story homes, debating whether to just slam on my brakes and confront him.

Finally, after about fifteen minutes of him riding my tail, I pull over and park in front of the curb. I half expect him to stop, but instead, he drives by really slowly with his baseball cap pulled low. Then he punches the gas and peels off down the road.

I try to catch his license plate number, but it's covered

in grime, so all I can do is take a mental note of the make and model of the vehicle.

"Maybe I'm just overreacting," I try to convince myself. "I mean, who in the hell would even be following me?"

I don't have an answer, but as I pull back onto the road, I can't shake the unsettling feeling stirring inside me that something isn't quite right.

THREE
CALLIE

"SO YOU JUST TOLD HER your entire life story?" my best friend Seth gapes at me as he sticks a spoon into the tub of cookie dough ice cream that's balanced on the couch cushion between us. In typical Seth fashion, he's dressed to impress, wearing a stylish pair of jeans, a button-down shirt with the sleeves rolled up, designer sneakers, and his highlighted hair is tousled in an intentionally messy way. "I can't believe it. Usually, I have to pry words out of you."

The moment I left the interview, I texted him, freaking out that I had ended up babbling my entire life story to Evie and he told me he'd meet me at my apartment ASAP.

It's not like I mind telling people about my past. I'm just usually not that much of a talker, nor do I go around telling everyone every detail about me and my past. It's not my style.

"See, this is why I think all interviews for writing jobs should be conducted through questionnaire forms." I shovel up a glob of partially melted ice cream, debating whether or not to turn the heater up. While it's sprint time, Laramie can get cold until summer arrives. "I'm a writer, which means I'm good at expressing myself in writing, not verbalizing." Sighing, I stuff the bite of ice cream into my mouth and let it melt on my tongue. "This stinks. I really wanted the job."

He licks his spoon clean. "Don't get too discouraged yet. You still might get it."

I get up and turn on the heater. "I talked for over an hour straight and even told her how I chopped my hair off after Caleb raped me. How on earth is that going to get me the job?"

He pats my hand as I sit back down. "Because your story's inspiring."

"Yeah, but inspiring doesn't scream: hire me for this job that requires a bunch of undercover work, some sketchy situations, and being creative and thinking outside of the box. It just says: hey, I have an inspiring story and some past issues."

"Just because you had issues doesn't make you any less qualified for a job. In fact, it shows that you're motivated and understand things not every person can. And your inspiring story makes you stand out in the sea of journalists all trying to nab your job."

"I don't know about that." I sigh, sinking back into the sofa. "Sadly, my story isn't that unique. Stuff like that happens to girls and women all the time. And even guys. It's horrible that things are that way. It really, really is."

It's something I've thought about a lot lately, all the news articles about rape victims and attacks. One of the worst parts is how often the attacker gets off easy. Like Caleb. While he was arrested for drug charges, he hasn't— and probably won't—actually be charged for the rapes he committed, for several different reasons. Because too much time had passed since he committed the crime. Because his victims were either too afraid to step forward or, like Luke's sister, had passed away. Because there wasn't enough evidence. The list goes on and on, and it drives me absolutely crazy when I think about it too much. It's part of the reason why I really want the job at *The Offbeat Go Daily*. They've done many articles on those sorts of topics and have even aided in a couple of arrests of criminals.

"Yes, it is," he agrees with a distant nod, his mind probably wandering back to his own sad story. Blinking a few times, he stabs the spoon into the tub of ice cream.

"Still, I don't think you should get upset just yet. Not until you know for sure if you got the job."

"I'm pretty sure I didn't. I mean, the last words she said to me were pretty ominous." I fiddle with the four leaf clover pendant hanging on the chain of the necklace I'm wearing. A pendant Kayden, my boyfriend, gave me because he thinks I'm lucky.

I sure wish it'd bring me some luck now.

His brow rises. "What'd she say?"

I shrug. "If she's interested, she'll be in touch."

He winces, but then quickly shakes the look off. "That's not too terrible."

"Then why'd you just wince?"

He itches his eye. "I didn't. My eye's been spasming all day."

I almost smile for the first time since I left the interview. "You're such a little liar."

"And you're such a little ice cream hog." He grabs the tub of ice cream and hugs it against his chest. "This thing was half full when I brought it over."

"Yeah and it was only half full because you ate half of it in the car." My smile breaks through. But I'm not surprised. Seth has always been talented at making me smile when I'm feeling gloomy.

He presses his hand to his chest, faking aghast. "I so did not. I'd never eat ice cream and drive."

"Then why were your hands all sticky when you showed up here?"

"How do you know my hands were sticky?"

"Because the fridge handle was sticky after you opened the fridge."

"Are you sure that wasn't from Kayden? I heard he likes to raid the freezer after you guys get your freak on."

"Ew, no." I playfully swat his arm, and he laughs. "And how would that even make the handle sticky?"

The wicked glint in his eyes makes me instantly regret asking the question.

"Never mind." I hold up my hand, my cheeks warming. "Forget I asked."

He chuckles, digging into the ice cream again. "You know, even after knowing you for almost two years, it's still amusing as fuck to make you blush."

"And even after knowing you for almost two years, it's still as amusing as... fuck to steal your ice cream." Then I steal his tub of ice cream and run out the front door, laughing my butt off.

"Hey!" he shouts, racing down the stairway after me. "Don't you dare eat any of that. I just got to a section that had a shit ton of cookie dough."

"I'm so going to!" I shout through my laughter as I reach the bottom of the stairway. Then I take off toward the carport, unsure where I'm going, but it's one of those moments where you don't really need a plan or direction. Or shoes, apparently, since I ran out barefoot. "Dang it." I hop around as the soles of my feet touch the freezing cold sidewalk. "That's freezing."

"It's going to be a lot colder when I dump that ice cream on your head!" Seth yells as he comes barreling down the stairway.

I reel around as I reach the curb. "Take one step closer, and the ice cream is going to become friends with the sidewalk."

He doesn't slow down. "Like you would dare waste a perfectly good tub of ice cream."

"Half of a tub," I correct. "And I would if it meant it'd stop you from dumping it on my head." Then, just to mess with him, I start to tip the tub of ice cream to the side.

He slows from a jog to a walk. "Callie Lawrence, don't you dare waste that."

Sometimes it's really fun teasing him. "What? This?" I angle it more to the side, not really planning on dumping any out. But then I jump as the icy concrete starts to burn against my feet and the movement sends a glob of ice cream out of the tub and to the ground.

Seth overdramatically gasps as he stares down at the splattered glob. "Oh my God, there was like three pieces of cookie dough in that."

I press my lips together, stifling a laugh. Deep down I

know he's only partially kidding—Seth really loves his ice cream. "I'm sorry. I didn't mean to actually spill it. I was just pretending, but then my feet got cold, and I jumped and... Well, yeah."

"Pretending or not, *that* still happened," he gestures at the ice cream on the ground.

"I know, but it was completely by accident. I swear." I draw an *x* over my heart with my finger.

"I'm not sure if I really believe you. In fact, I'm pretty sure you've secretly held a food vendetta against me ever since I accidentally ate all of your peppermint bark. And you threatened to get me back for that."

"That's because it's only available around Christmas-time. And I was just kidding about getting you back." Sort of.

He crosses his arms and sticks his nose up in the air. "I don't believe you."

I can't help but laugh. "Fine, if it's that big of a deal, I'll give you your ice cream back." I step forward and offer him the tub.

The moment he takes it, a Cheshire grin takes over his face. "I'm so the best friend *ever*. I mean, I got you to smile and relax and not think about that job. I think I should get like the best friend ever award or something."

I give him a hug. "Thank you for being the best friend in the whole wide world."

He chuckles, giving me a one-armed hug. "And thank you for being you, baby girl. And I have a feeling you might get the job. And even if you don't, I know you'll be hired for another one that's equally as great."

"Because you're psychic?" I ask through a laugh.

"You know it." He pulls back, grinning. "And I'm the smartest person ever."

"Yes, you are—" I squeal like a wild banshee as a pair of arms loop around my waist and lift me up from the ground. The next thing I know I'm being slung over a broad shoulder and my pulse speeds up in a panic.

But my heart settles as the scent of Kayden's cologne touches my nostrils.

Seth busts up laughing as he walks around and tips his head to the side, looking at me hanging upside down. "Holy shit, that noise you made was classic." He digs into the ice cream with his fingers, picks out a chunk of cookie dough, and pops it into his mouth. "Seriously, I think you could give me a run for my money with that squeal of terror."

I narrow my eyes at him as Kayden chuckles and lightly pinches me on the butt. "The next time we're watching a scary movie, I'm going to record you screaming at every scary part and then make the video go viral."

Seth's eyes widen. "Now that's just plain cruel."

"Okay, maybe it is a little bit," I admit. "But still... You could've at least warned me that Kayden was sneaking up on me."

He shrugs. "Now where's the fun in that?"

Kayden chuckles. "Glad to see Seth got you out of your funk."

"I wasn't in a funk... Was I?" I lift my head and look questioningly at Seth.

He offers me an apologetic look as he nods. "Sorry, but you were. That's okay, though. We're all allowed to have our grumpy days. Just know, though, that you only get one a week."

I nod, sweeping my hair out of my face. "Yes, sir."

He chuckles as he backs away. "I'm going to head home now since your prince charming is here. Call me if you need anything." He turns on his heels, calling over his shoulder, "Have fun making sticky, refrigerator handle messes, you two."

"Sticky refrigerator handle messes... What does that..." Kayden shakes his head. "Nope, never mind. With you two it's usually better not to ask." He starts for the stairway with me still draped over his shoulder.

"Are you going to carry me all the way up?" I ask through a giggle.

"All the way into our bedroom where I'll spend all night cheering you up." He pinches my butt again, and I laugh.

But then something dawns on me.

"Wait. I thought you had practice tonight?"

"I did, but I messaged Coach and told him I was sick."

"But there's a game tomorrow."

"Yeah, so. I can miss one practice every once in a while, especially when my girlfriend needs cheering up." He holds onto the back of my thighs as he ascends up the stairway.

"I don't want you missing practice just because I'm having a bad day." I clutch onto the back of his jacket as I start to slip off his shoulder.

He tightens his grip on me. "Yeah, so? I'm not worried and neither should you be. I kick ass."

"I know you kick ass," I say, and he chuckles at my use of a swear word, something he usually does. "I just don't want to mess anything up for you."

"You never mess up anything for me." He pushes open the door to our apartment. "You always bring me good luck. And you should know that by now." He gently lowers me off his shoulder and releases me when my feet touch the carpet. Then his hands instantly find my cheeks and he cups my face between his palms. "Now, are you going to explain what got you upset to begin with, why you and Seth were running around outside with a tub of ice cream, and why on earth you aren't wearing any shoes when it's forty degrees outside?"

I sneak a quick look and take him all in; his sturdy body, the way his brown hair falls into his green, loving eyes that light up every time he sees me. I sometimes still can't believe I'm with him, that I was able to get past the darkness of my past enough to trust him to bring me into the light.

"We were fighting over his ice cream, so I took off outside with it. Forgot to put on my shoes. As for being upset, it was mostly because I'm pretty sure I messed up the job interview." I sigh. "Honestly, I feel like sort of a baby. I mean, it's just a job, right?"

He skims his thumb along the bottom of my eye. "You have every right to be upset. I know how much you wanted that job. But..." He removes his hands from my face and threads his fingers through mine. "I don't think you should get upset until you know for sure you didn't get it."

"I'll try, but I'm about ninety-nine percent sure I didn't get it."

His brow curves upward. "That still leaves one percent. And I think when it comes to odds and percentages, you and I can beat just about anything."

"I see your point."

"Good, because my points are usually awesome." His lips quirk. "Now, how about I make you dinner and you tell me about your day."

Deciding there's no use sulking over something that hasn't happened yet, I stand on my tiptoes and loop my arms around the back of his neck. "Actually, I spent the last hour talking about my day to Seth and I'm feeling pretty talked out."

"Oh yeah?"

"Yeah."

A naughty glint twinkles in his eyes. "So what do you think we should do then?"

Instead of answering him with words, I seal my lips to his. His hands slide down and cup my butt. Then he pushes me closer and parts my lips with his tongue, devouring me with a kiss.

"God, I miss this," he murmurs between kisses. "Kissing you at five o'clock in the afternoon when I'm still wide awake and not about to pass out."

"If you want, I can start stopping by before practice to give you a kiss," I tease, threading my fingers through his hair.

"I might take you up on that offer." He kisses me deeply then pulls back a sliver of an inch. "Now, no more talking."

Before I can ask why, he scoops me up and urges my legs around his waist. Then he kisses me again as he carries me to the sofa and sits down with me straddling his waist. I pull back, but only long enough to peel his shirt off and quickly trace my fingers along the scars covering his chest. Scars that remind me of his horrible past and how far he's come since the day he and I first connected.

"My turn," he whispers when my fingers reach his collarbone.

I lean back and raise my arms above my head so he can pull off my shirt. Then he unclasps my bra and begins to explore my body like I just did with him. Once he's felt almost every inch of me, we peel off the rest of our clothes and reunite our lips as he slips inside me.

He groans as he grips my hips. "God, I'll never get tired of this."

"Me either," I agree, clutching onto his shoulders.

He rocks his hips against mine, and my eyes roll into the back of my head as I move with him, both of us pushing each other toward bliss. Away from reality. Away from the everyday worries of life. Because that's what Kayden and I do for each other. We make things better when we're together. We make chaos easier to deal with when we're together.

And I truly believe that together, there isn't anything we can't take on.

TWO HOURS LATER, Kayden and I are dressed and

lying on the sofa. Or well, we're half dressed; me in his shirt and him in his boxers. I'm exhausted. Beyond beat. But feel way better than I did earlier today. So, when there's a knock on the door, I make no move to get up.

"I don't want to answer that," I murmur as I rest my head on his chest. "I'm too comfortable.

Kayden plays with my hair. "Who do you think it is?"

I shrug through a yawn. "I'm sure no one important. If it was, they probably would've texted first." I laugh to myself. "Or maybe it's my mom. Maybe she lost her mind completely and drove up here to bug me."

He laughs softly. "Is she still bugging you about getting married ?"

I nod as he skims his fingertip along the top of my engagement ring. "I've tried to explain to her at least a dozen times that it's not a huge deal that we're living together without being married, but you know how she can get." I nuzzle closer to him. "She's so old school sometimes."

"Yeah, she is." He kisses the top of my head.

The person knocks on the door again. And again, I make no effort to get up, but I do note that Kayden's chest muscles wind tight.

I push up to look him in the eyes. "Is something wrong? It seemed like you just tensed up."

"It's nothing," he promises, but confusion crosses his

expression. "It's just that when I was headed home today, I thought this SUV was following me, so eventually I pulled over. He just drove by, though, so I think I was being paranoid."

"How far did he follow you for?"

"Well, I turned off into a subdivision to see if I could lose him. I drove around in there for a bit before finally pulling over."

"That's really weird."

"I know, but I'm sure it's nothing to worry about. I mean, why would anyone be following me?"

"Maybe you have a stalker football fan," I tease. Well, partially tease. The truth is, what he told me has me a bit concerned.

"Maybe." He gives me a quick kiss. "Let's not worry about it right now. I'm sure it was nothing—"

Knock. Knock. Knock.

The knocks are louder this time, as if the person is announcing they aren't going to give up anytime soon.

Sighing, I climb off Kayden and move to pull on my jeans so I can answer the door. But he gets to his feet and reaches for his shirt.

"Let me answer it, okay?" A nervous edge creeps into his tone.

He might be trying to play off this SUV following him

thing, but it's fairly clear he's nervous, which makes me wonder who he thinks could be following him.

I nod but still pull on my jeans while he slips on his pants. Then he crosses the room and throws open the door just as the knocking starts up again.

"Who are you?" Kayden says to whoever is outside.

I move over to get a better look and my lips part in shock.

Standing outside on the porch is the secretary from *The Offbeat Go Daily*, who I learned before I left my interview is named Easton. He has on the same outfit as he did earlier along with a leather jacket and fingerless gloves.

"Hey, Callie." Easton greets me with a smile.

"Um, hey." I scratch my head, confused why he's here while Kayden glances at me with his brow arched.

He smiles at Kayden's confusion. "I'm sure you're probably confused why I'm here."

I nod. "Yeah, pretty much."

"Good. I think that's why Evie does it like this. She likes to keep her workers on their toes." He winks at me.

Kayden no longer appears perplexed but kind of irritated. "Who are you again?" he asks.

Easton tears his gaze off me and offers Kayden his hand. "I'm Easton. I work for Evie at *The Offbeat Go Daily*.

"I'm Kayden, Callie's boyfriend." Kayden shakes his hand, and I detect a wince on Easton's part. "Don't take this the wrong way, but why are you standing on our doorstep at eight o'clock at night?"

"It's a little weird, isn't it?" Easton agrees as he lets go of Kayden's hand then reaches into his pocket. "Evie likes to do things a little unconventionally, though." His gaze lands on me. "Something you've probably already figured out by now." When I nod, he removes his hand from his pocket. His fingers are wrapped around what looks like a present. Even a bow decorates the top. "This is for you." He hands me the present in question.

I take it and fiddle with the bow. "What's in it?"

"A present. Obviously." His lips quirk. "Well, that is, if you still want the job. If not, I guess it's just a thing wrapped up in a bunch of decorative paper that you're probably going to throw out when I leave."

I have literally never been more lost in my entire life. Does this mean I got the job? What on earth is inside this present? And why is Evie having Easton deliver me presents at all?

I give the present a little shake, eliciting a laugh from Easton. "Should I open it now?"

He shakes his head. "Wait for me to leave first."

"Why..." I start to ask, but he's already walking away.

"See you hopefully sooner rather than later, Callie," he calls over his shoulder.

Kayden shuts the door and turns to me with his brows raised. "That's the secretary at this place you want to work at?"

I nod as I pick at the edge of the wrapping paper. "I know he doesn't really look like a typical secretary, but the whole place was pretty atypical." I sit down on the edge of the sofa. "You should've seen Evie's office. Her entire wall was covered with her research. I've never seen anything so crazy. Or old school, I guess."

Kayden sits down beside me and nods at the present in my hand. "So does this mean you got the job?"

"I'm not sure." But I'm sure whatever is inside this present might give me an idea.

My stomach bubbles with excitement and nervousness.

"But if you got the job, you'd be working with that Easton guy, right?" he asks.

I shrug, tearing off the bow. "I have no idea. Evie didn't tell me a lot of the details about the job, which is part of the reason why I was pretty certain I wasn't getting hired." I glance up and find him staring at me with a frown on his face and a crease between his brows. "What's wrong?" I smooth my finger between his brows, erasing his worry lines.

"It's nothing." He shrugs, staring down at his hands.

I tilt my head to the side to meet his gaze. "It is something, or else you wouldn't have that frown on your face."

He sighs, lifting his gaze to me. "I'm just thinking about some stuff I have to do tomorrow that's stressing me out."

I'm almost certain he's lying, but when I start to open my mouth to encourage him to talk to me, he places a finger against my lips.

"I promise I'm fine." He lowers his finger and smiles. "Now open your present."

He can pretend all he wants, but I can tell when something is bothering him. I make a mental note to bring it up later then rip the wrapping paper off. Inside is a box with a lid and inside that is a notebook with my name embroidered onto the front, a pen decorated with skulls, a key, and a card.

I pick up the card and read the note.

Callie Lawrence,

I'd like to officially welcome you to The Offbeat Go Daily team. That is if you accept my job offer. Inside this box, there should be a notebook and a pen because, as you probably already figured out, I like old school research methods. There should also be a key. Bring that with you tonight when you meet me at the bookshop on Main Road Drive and Autumn Breeze Way at ten o'clock. Again, that is if you decide to accept my job offer. You don't need to dress up. We're not doing anything fancy. Just discussing some details.

And please, don't be late. It's very important.

--Evie

PS: I really do hope you accept the job. I think you'd be perfect for it.

To say I'm surprised would be a complete understatement. During the interview, Evie had seemed less than impressed by me. But I guess I misinterpreted her indifference.

"You got the job then?" Kayden asks, looking up from the card.

"I think so." I set the card down and pull out the notebook and pen.

"And you're excited, right?" He watches me carefully. "Because you seem a little subdued right now."

"I'm just a little confused," I admit, fanning through the blank notebook pages. "I really didn't think I was going to get hired."

"I figured you would."

"How? You weren't even there."

He kisses my cheek. "Because anyone who speaks to you for more than a couple of minutes realizes how perfect you are."

A smile touches my lips. "As much as I love you for saying that, that's completely untrue."

"Nope. I never lie." He presses a kiss to my lips. "And I'm always right."

I laugh against his mouth. "You're starting to sound like Seth."

He playfully pinches my side, and I let out a squeal as I laugh.

"That's not a bad thing!" I cry through my laughter as he softly pinches me again.

"I don't know about that. Seth's a little weirdo." He leans over me, forcing me to lie down on my back, then pins my head between his arms. "So, are you taking the job? Because you never said for sure if you are."

I nod. "I think I'd regret it if I didn't. And I have a feeling it's going to turn out amazing. At least, I hope so."

"I'm sure it will." He kisses me again then hops off and pats me on the butt. "Now go hit the shower and get ready."

I giggle as I push to my feet. "Yes, coach."

He smacks my ass again then wraps his arms around me, his chest pressing against my back. "Better yet, I think I'll hit the shower with you."

Then he flings me over his shoulder and carries me into the bathroom where we pick up right where we left off before Easton knocked on the door. But even through the kisses and the touches, my nerves continue to build. While I want the job and am super excited, it seems a bit strange that I have to meet up with Evie at the bookshop at ten o'clock at night. What could we possibly be doing at a bookshop that late? I didn't even realize bookshops stayed open that late. I wonder if this is a normal thing with this job. I wonder if I'll be able to handle it.

I guess I'm about to find out.

FOUR
KAYDEN

CALLIE IS beyond nervous as she gathers her stuff so she can meet her new boss. It's ridiculously amusing watching her shuffle around our apartment, flustered, and nervous. I'm sure she'll probably act this way until she gets used to the job, which is fine. While I'm happy for her, I can't help but be a bit unsettled by the way that Easton secretary dude was openly flirting with her in front of me. Sure, Callie was completely clueless about it, and even if she wasn't, I know she'd never cheat on me. But the guy flirted with her right in front of me, even when he knew I was her boyfriend and that doesn't sit well with me.

I'm not about to bring this up, though. Tonight is about her, and all I need to do right now is be excited.

"How do I look?" she asks for the tenth time in the last five minutes.

She's wearing a pair of black jeans and a red top that matches her clunky velvet boots. Her hair is braided to the side, and she's put on some black liner around her eyes, and I think a bit of lipstick.

"You look..." I tilt my head to the side and let my gaze scroll over her body. "Hot, actually."

Her cheeks flush. "I do not."

"Actually, you kind of do." I tuck a stray strand of her hair behind her ear. "Relax. You look perfect. You always do."

"You say that too much to me." She leans into my touch, staring up at me with those big, beautiful eyes of hers. "But thank you for saying it."

It's moments like these, when she's looking at me like I'm her entire world, that make me feel so whole inside. There's nowhere else I'd rather be, and I'm so fucking grateful she continues to want to be with me.

"I say it because I mean it." I lightly graze my lips across hers, and she sighs contently against my mouth.

"I should probably get going," she murmurs. "The note said not to be late."

"Okay." I lean back, sweeping my knuckles across her cheek. "Do you want me to drive you?"

Shaking her head, she collects her car keys and the notebook and pen Evie gave her. "I don't want to make you wait around. I'm not even sure how long I'm going to be."

"I don't mind waiting." Plus, I don't like the idea of her driving around this late by herself.

While Callie takes kickboxing classes and carries a can of pepper spray in her purse, I'm always nervous whenever she's out late by herself. Both of us know too well about the evils hidden in the world. Plus, that whole guy following me around has me on edge.

"It's okay. You have a game tomorrow anyway. You need your rest." She stands on her tiptoes to kiss me goodbye, pulling away too soon.

I press my hand to the small of her back and guide her back to my lips. "Promise me you'll message me when you get there and when you leave, okay?" I seal my lips to hers, parting her lips with my tongue and kissing us both breathless. "And let me walk you to your car."

She nods easily. Walking her to the car is something I do every time she goes out late.

Threading my fingers through her's, we head outside into the cold night. My gaze instinctively scans the parking lot that's lit up by a few lampposts. I'm not even sure what I'm looking for. Maybe nothing. And that's pretty much what I see—nothing except a few other people wandering out to their cars. Still, my nerves are all over the place tonight, as if I can sense something unsettling heading my way. The last time I felt like this my dad died.

"Be safe," I tell Callie as she unlocks the car door.

"I will. And I love you." She climbs into the car, nervousness written all over her face

"I love you too." I grab the door as she starts to shut it. "Hey, you're going to do great. They wouldn't have gone through all of this trouble to tell you that you got the job if they weren't impressed by you."

She chews on her bottom lip. "I just hope I do well with... Well, whatever this thing is tonight."

"You will. You're an amazing writer and person." Then, just because I can, I steal another kiss from her.

"You're amazing too." She smiles at me then closes the door.

She says that to me all the time, but it still blows my mind that she sees me as amazing.

I stand in the parking lot and watch her drive away, only heading back inside when her taillights disappear down the road. I'm halfway to the stairs, my thoughts stuck in Callie Land, when I hear someone call out my name.

"Kayden Owens?"

I glance around then promptly tense as I spot the guy who was following me earlier slowly walking across the grass. He's wearing the same outfit as he had on before only he's ditched the hat and has the sleeves of his shirt rolled up.

"Can I help you?" I cross my arms and stare him down, trying to be as intimidating as I can.

"I'm hoping so." He comes to a stop in front of me. "You are Kayden Owens, right?"

"That all depends on who wants to know."

"I..." He glances at a couple exiting their apartment. "Can we go somewhere and talk privately?"

"No," I say flatly. "Whatever you have to say, you can do it right here, man."

He's really starting to creep me out. While I can hold my own in a fight, he's not a small guy. He's at least as tall as me with the same type of build, so there's a fifty-fifty chance I'll be able to kick his ass if I need to. I hate fighting, though. It reminds me too much of my psychopath of a father.

He surrenders his hands in front of him. "I swear I'm not trying to come off weird. I just really want to talk to you. *Need* to actually."

"Well, your efforts at trying not to be creepy are failing because you're acting fucking weird as hell."

He chuckles, his hands falling to his sides. "I guess I probably am, huh?"

"And speaking of creepy. Did you follow me earlier today?" The fact that he knows where I live has to mean he did. Realizing that, I turn to leave. "You know what. You need to leave before I call the police."

"Kayden wait." He rushes after me, but I only quicken my pace. "Please just listen to me. I promise what I have to say is important." He jogs to my side. "It's about your father... He wants to talk to you."

I slam to a stop so swiftly he nearly trips over his feet. "Nice try but my father is dead," I bite out, more than pissed off.

"Not the father who raised you," he says with pity in his eyes. "Your real father."

"Fuck you," I spit out then I rush up the stairwell and lock myself in my apartment.

The guy knocks on the door several times, yammering about how my birth father wants to meet me. Eventually he gives up and leaves, but not before slipping a card underneath the door.

I don't pick it up as I pace the living room, my thoughts racing a million miles a minute. What if what he said is true? What if my father wasn't my birth father? What if all those years of abuse were never supposed to be my real life?

I want to tear the card to pieces. I want to scream. What I really want to do is cut the pain right out of me.

FIVE

CALLIE

BY THE TIME I pull up to the bookshop, I have about fifteen minutes before I'm supposed to meet Evie. But I guess being early is better than being late. I'd go inside to wait for her except all the lights are off in the bookshop and no one appears to be inside.

"Is it closed?" I look around for a sign that announces so, but can't spot one anywhere.

Wanting to know the hours of when it's open, I do a quick search on the Internet about the bookshop, but nothing comes up.

"So weird." I drum my fingers on top of the steering wheel, unsure of what else to do. I don't have Evie's personal number, or Easton's, only the office's.

I decide to give the office a quick call, but no one answers. The only option that leaves me is to wait around for a bit and see if anyone shows up. I still have ten more minutes until ten o'clock anyway.

After I make sure the doors are all locked, I relax back in the seat and text Kayden that I've made it to the bookshop. It may be a Friday night, but this side of the town is dead, only a few other cars are parked on the side of the road, and none of the stores are open. The desolation makes me uneasy. I hate that it does. Hate that I can't feel safe sitting in my car. But that's the world we live in today, unfortunately.

Five minutes later, no one has shown up yet and strangely, Kayden hasn't texted me back. Unless he's at practice, he never takes more than a few minutes to reply, especially when I'm out and about alone and he asks that I check in. I'm about to call him, mostly because I'm bored, when I receive a message from Violet, Luke's girlfriend, who I've grown kind of close to.

Violet: Hey! Are we still on for Halloween costume shopping tomorrow?

Me: Of course! We can't break tradition!

Back around Halloween, her, Seth, and I all went shopping together for costumes. We had a lot of fun and bonded over helping each other pick out costumes. Since then it's become a tradition that we go together, and I like that we do. Like that I have traditions with my friends. Like that I have friends.

Violet: Awesome. Are you driving or me?

Me: I think we should make Seth. He never does.

Violet: I'm down for that. Let's make him buy coffee too. He makes us do it every time we go out.

Me: Sounds like a plan to me.

Violet: You want to message him or should I?

Me: Lol, I'll do it. You two are too sassy to take orders from each other.

Violet: Hey, I'm not sassy. I'm just opinionated.

I'm about to respond when a light tap sounds on my window, startling me so badly I drop my phone. When my head snaps up, I relax.

Evie smiles at me through the passenger side window. "Sorry, I didn't mean to startle you."

"It's fine." I lean over to pick up my phone off the floor. "I was just in my own little world and didn't see you walk up."

She motions for me to get out of the car. "Come on inside, and let's talk."

I quickly gather my stuff and hop out of the car while she proceeds to unlock the front door to the bookshop. "Do you own the place?" I ask as I move up beside her.

"I do." She nudges open the door and steps inside, wiggling the key from the lock. "The location is great. Nice and empty—where we can have a lot of privacy."

I nod like I understand what she's talking about, but really, I'm lost. Don't most business owners want a location that will drive in more customers?

But I soon find out the reason behind her statement as she locks the door back up then leads me to the back of the store, beyond the dusty bookshelves, and to a door in the far back that's secured with three deadbolts.

"Now, I have to warn you about what's on the other side of this door," she says as she begins working on unlocking the locks. "We're not your average, run of the mill news agency. We like our journalists to get deep inside the stories. Like I told you in the interview, we pride ourselves on being in-depth and for occasionally solving cases. In fact, we prefer that our research can lead to arrests." She's on the second to last lock now, and my heart is thundering inside my chest. I don't even know why, or what I think is going to be on the other side of that door. "But if people found out that's what we're about, we'd have a more complicated time going under-cover, so most of what we do here at *Offbeat* remains a secret. We also like our journalists not to use their real names while they're getting a scoop on a story." She doesn't unlock the final lock, instead dropping the keys into her purse and digging out an envelope. "This is for you to read and sign. Once you sign, I'll explain more to you."

Setting my bag down on a shelf, I take the envelope from her and open it. Inside is a non-disclosure agreement, which isn't too strange. After reading through it, I dig the pen out that Evie gave me and sign my name at the bottom.

"Awesome." She takes the paper from me and puts it into her bag. "Do you have that key I gave you?"

"Yes." I grab it from my bag and hold it up. "Right here."

"Good. Now put it in the final lock and unlock the door."

This is by far the strangest thing I've ever experienced on a job, but I do as instructed and stick the key into the final lock and unlock the door.

"That key opens all the locks, including the one on the front door to the bookshop," Evie explains as her fingers wrap around the doorknob. "If you choose to accept the offer I'm about to make you, you get to keep the key and use this place whenever you need it. Just make sure to always keep the door locked whether you're staying or leaving. All of our research is locked up in here, and we don't want anyone wandering in and finding it." With that, she opens the door.

After such a build-up of anticipation, I half expect there to be some sort of futuristic, computerized room on the other side. But nope. It's just a normal room with cluttered desks, computers, a coffee station, and, like at Evie's office, research is tacked to the walls. A few people are typing away at computers, but no one looks up when I enter.

"I'll make introductions later if you decide you want the job," Evie explains as she leads me across the room and into a small, wall-enclosed area crammed with a desk, a filing cabinet, and a few computers. She plops down in a chair and signals for me to do the same. "Please, have a seat."

I do as she instructs, sit down, and put my bag on my lap. I know I should be asking questions, but all of this—secret rooms, the package Easton delivered to me—it's struck me speechless.

"You've been pretty quiet," Evie states as she turns on her computer. "Have I scared you off already?"

I shake my head. "I'm just trying to process all of this."

"It's a lot to take in, isn't it?"

"Yeah," I admit truthfully. "I guess I'm just trying to figure out why the need for so much secrecy."

"That's actually the perfect opening for me to

explain what I'd like your first job to be." She double clicks the mouse then turns the computer screen toward me.

On the screen is a photo of a battered girl maybe a year or two younger than me. Her eyes are swollen, her cheek is bruised, and her top lip is split open. Her eyes, though, are what shatter my soul. So hollow. So familiar. Like staring into a mirror almost a decade ago.

My gut twists as my mind conjures up images of what could have happened to her. "Who is she?"

"I can't give out her name to you just yet. Not until I know you're in," Evie explains, watching me assess the photo. "But this photo is one of many. The victims, they all have a few of the same traits. They were all beaten and raped at a party. They can't remember much about what happened, which probably means they were drugged, and they're all being blackmailed into silence. Or are too scared to go to the police." She faces me and overlaps her hands on her desk. "I know one of the victims—that's how I was able to find out this was going on and get some information on this. But no one's been able to figure out who's behind the attacks."

"Haven't the police looked into it?"

"Most of the women won't go to the police, because of the blackmail and the fear and shame they feel. The only reason we have information on them and photos is that some of them took the photos themselves to have proof if they ever decided to come forward."

"That makes sense. I mean, about being too scared and ashamed to come forward." Sadly, silence is something I understand all too well. I had let the silence own me for years, let the secrets eat away at my soul. It was when I spoke up that I finally freed myself from the self-torment and self-blame. Knowing what I know now, I wish I'd spoken up sooner. "Maybe you could go to the police and show them these photos."

"I wish it were that easy, but unless the victims come forward, I can't do much. And I think, considering what you told me in our interview, you understand that even if I did go to the police, there's a chance the case might not get anywhere."

"Yeah, sadly I do understand that." I rub my lips together, contemplating. "So, is this the story you want me to write about? About these girls and their attacks?"

The idea makes me nervous, mostly because their stories will be so connected to my past. Sure, I've dealt with what happened to me, but I worry it could trigger past emotions inside me.

She shakes her head, confusing me even more. "I don't just want you to write about their story, Callie. I want you to figure it out and get justice."

I blink at her. "You want me to figure out who raped these girls?"

"I want you to *try*," she emphasizes. "I want you to get deep into the story. I want you to understand it and make others understand it. But most of all, I want justice for the victims."

I pick at a loose thread on the seam of my pants. "I want justice for them too. I really do. But... But I'm just a girl in college who wants to be a journalist. I'm not a detective, and this sounds more like a thing for a detective."

She smiles as if she expected that answer. "The last places you worked for—they were all about the story, right?" she asks, and I nod. "Well, *Offbeat* isn't about that. We're about getting justice through the story. If we weren't, we'd be like almost every other news column out there, putting our words down and telling the world, but not really doing anything to change it." She leans forward, her eyes bursting with the sort of excitement I wish I could feel at the moment, but honestly, I'm scared shitless. "Change the world, Callie. I know you have it in you. Otherwise you wouldn't be here."

"I want to." Man, do I. I've thought about it so much. "But... it sounds sort of dangerous."

"It is, but that's why we'll be pairing you up with a partner. They'll also show you the ropes of *Offbeat*." She doesn't even try to sugarcoat it. "I don't want to frighten you off, but danger kind of comes with the territory of being a really good journalist who writes about important things. All of the best journalists I know don't just tell the story, they live and breathe it until it etches into their soul. They feel it. Experience it. It's what makes a truly good story."

Her words are powerful—they really are—but again, and for reasons I can't even quite understand yet, I hesitate.

I smooth my hands along the tops of my legs. "But it's not just about the story, right? It's also about getting justice."

"You catch on quickly." She reclines back in her chair. "I know this is something you probably need to think about—it's a really big decision—so why don't you go home and think about it for the night? You can let me know tomorrow if you want the job. If not, no hard feelings. I promise." She gives a short pause. "I really hope you do, though. With your background, I think you could really connect with this story and the victims in a way not everyone could."

I nod. "Okay, I will."

We chat for a few more minutes then she walks me out of the store. As I'm pulling out onto the road, I spot two girls around my age walking down the sidewalk. Just a ways behind them are a group of guys yelling at them and laughing. With my windows rolled up, I can't tell what they're saying, but with how fast the girls are walking, I'm betting they're not nice and comforting words.

I drive down the street slowly until the girls make it a safe distance away, then I press on the gas and head home to talk to Kayden about what happened tonight. Because if there's one person in this world that can help me make a decision like this, it's him.

SIX

KAYDEN

WHEN CALLIE ARRIVES HOME, she finds me sitting on the kitchen floor with a couple of empty beer bottles beside me.

"Kayden." Worry laces her tone as she rushes across the living room, her bag falling to the floor as she crouches down in front of me. "What happened?"

I shake my head, still completely dumbstruck at what the guy told me. "I don't even know." I draw my knees up and lower my head into my hands.

"Hey, talk to me." Her fingers wrap around my wrists, and then her gaze skims along the fresh cut on the side of my arm.

"It's not what you think," I murmur. "I dropped a beer, and while I was picking up the glass, I accidentally cut myself." It's the truth too. "I'm not going to lie, though.

I thought about it. Cutting myself..." It's been so long since I had the urge to do it. I forgot how overwhelming the compulsion could be. But picturing Callie's face helped me talk myself out of doing it.

"That's good you didn't." Her voice is so gentle, so Callie. "Do you want to talk about what happened? What set it off?"

"Not really. But I probably need to." Sighing, I raise my head from my hands.

The moment our gazes connect, I start telling her everything that happened from the moment she left tonight. By the time I'm done, I feel a little better, but mostly I'm a confused mess.

She sits down on the floor in front of me and combs her fingers through my hair. "Do you think this guy was telling the truth?"

"I'm not sure. I don't know why he'd lie about something like that, though." I hand her the card he slipped underneath the door. "He left this."

She skims over the card. "Is this his card? Because if so, it means he works for a private detective agency."

I shrug. "I'm guessing it's his."

She traces her thumb along the side of the card with her thinking face on. "He didn't look familiar or anything?" she asks, and I shake my head. She pats the card against the palm of her hand. "Let me do a search about the agency online and see what comes up." She rises to her feet. "You don't have to, but I really think you should call your brother and see if he knows anything about this. Or if he can get in touch with your mom and see what she knows." Remorse fills her eyes at the mention of my mom, who I no longer speak to.

Pushing to my feet, I nod. "I'll see if Dylan's still up." Because I know that's the brother she meant I should call.

A few months ago, Tyler dropped off the face of the earth and no one has heard from him since. Sadly, none of us were too surprised. Until then, he had relapsed quite a bit with his drug addiction and would disappear for days on end. I've always felt sorry for him and wonder if he uses drugs as a way to deal with what dad put us through. Or, well my fake dad, if what the guy told me is true. And what about Dylan and Tyler? Does this apply to them too?

Suddenly, I'm more motivated to call Dylan than I was before. Digging my phone out of my pocket, I dial his number while Callie wanders off to our bedroom to grab her laptop.

"Hey," Dylan answers after four rings, and I can tell that I've woken him up. "You're up late."

"Yeah, sorry. I wasn't even paying attention to the time," I tell him as I move to the living room and sit down on the sofa.

"Is everything okay?" he asks. "Because you sound upset."

"I don't know." I massage my temple with my free hand, letting my eyelids slip shut. *Come on Kayden, just spit it out. There's no use dragging it out.* "Some guy stopped by today. I think he works for a private investigation agency or something. And he told me that... That Dad wasn't my birth father. And I was wondering if you knew anything about it."

"Holy shit," he breathes out. "Are you kidding me right now?"

"No." And I'm not sure if I want to find out. I'm unsure if I want it to be true.

I mean, what if this guy is worse than the man I thought was my real father? After all, he waited until I was almost twenty-two before tracking me down.

"Holy shit," he repeats. "Do you think he was telling the truth?"

"I'm not sure... I ran off before I could ask him any questions. He left a card, though." I rub my hand across my forehead. "I wanted to call you first before I call this guy up and see if you knew anything about it."

"I don't," he assures me. "If I did, I would've told you."

"So no one's visited you and told you the same thing?"

"No. But I've been out of town for the last couple of weeks, so, I don't know..." he curses again. "Fuck, this is some crazy shit. And... And what if it's true? What if our asshole of a father isn't really your dad?" He blows out a breath. "What're you going to do?"

"I don't know," I whisper, squeezing my eyes shut. "Callie's looking up stuff about the agency online right now. After I find out if it's a legit place, I'll go from there."

"Do you need me to come out there? Because I can."

"Maybe."

"Well, let me know... I want to be there for you like I wasn't in the past."

No matter how hard I try to convince Dylan what happened with Dad wasn't his fault, he still blames himself.

"It's not your fault," I still make an attempt to convince him. "But I promise I'll let you know if I need you to fly out here."

"Good." He drags out a pause. "I hate to bring this up, but I feel like I should because it could help you get some answers." He hesitates again. "Do you want me to call Mom and see what she knows about this?"

I figured that was where he was going. "You know how to contact her then?"

"I haven't talked to her in a while, but as far as I know, she still has the same number."

"I don't... I think..." I skim my finger along the fresh wound on the side of my arm. When the glass cut me, I felt a drop of relief from the confusion and pain stirring inside me. If I don't take care of this problem, I'll more than likely want to feel that relief again. And I don't want to go back to that dark place. Or drag Callie there with me. "Yeah, can you call her up? That is if you don't mind."

"It's the least I can do," he says. "I'll call her first thing in the morning."

"Thanks."

"Of course. It's what I'm here for."

We talk for a few more minutes than we say goodbye and hang up. Usually, we talk for longer but it's fucking late and honestly, my mind is too crammed with other shit to be much of a conversationalist.

By the time I've gotten off the phone, Callie has returned to the living room with a worried look on her face.

"The agency seems legit." She moves in front of me and takes my hand. "I think, if you want to, we should give them a call tomorrow."

Nodding, I wrap my fingers around her waist and guide her down so she's straddling my lap. "Thank you. Not just for looking that up, but for being here for me."

"You don't need to thank me. I love being here for you, just like you're always here for me." She softly kisses my lips. "I wish you would've called me, though, when that guy showed up. I would've come home."

"That's exactly why I didn't." I draw her with me as I lean back on the sofa. "Now, how about you take my mind off this whole dad ordeal and tell me how the meeting went?"

Her face contorts in puzzlement. "I'm not sure if I'm going to take the job or not."

I brush my knuckles along her cheek. "Why not?"

She shrugs, her face contorting even more. "I don't know if I can do it or not."

"Callie, if there's one thing I'm sure of in this world, it's that you can do anything you put your mind to."

Hesitancy crosses her expression. "You might want to hear what the job entails first before you give me a pep talk."

I frown. "You make it sound like it's something bad."

"It's not bad. In fact, it could be really, really good." She nibbles on her bottom lip. "But it could also be a little bit dangerous."

I immediately want to tell her not to do it, but that's not the sort of relationship we have. While I want to protect her in every way possible, it's not my place to tell her what she can and cannot do. She's smart. Whatever she decides will be the right decision.

"Can I tell you about it?" she asks quietly. "Maybe you can help me decide."

I nod, grateful she wants my opinion. Of course, when

she starts telling me about the job, I want to beg her not to take it. But again, that's not the kind of person I want to be —the kind who tells his girlfriend not to take a job because it makes him uneasy.

"It does sound kind of dangerous," I say after she's finished giving me a recap of how the meeting went.

She nods, leaning back a bit. "It also hits really close to home, and that scares me." She sighs. "But, there's this other part of me that's really excited about doing this. If I do it right, I could really do something that means something, you know."

"Whatever you decide, I'll support you." My chest tightens a bit. "But promise me you'll be careful. I couldn't handle losing you." I pull her closer to me. "You're my person, you know." Callie is everything to me, and I don't even want to think about what would happen if I lost her.

"You're my person too." She rests her forehead against mine. "I promise I'll be careful if I take the job, but you have to promise me that you'll keep me in the loop about everything that goes on with this whole dad thing. I don't want you not calling me just because you think I'm doing something more important." She leans back to look me in the eye. "Nothing is more important than you. Got it?"

I nod, the corners of my lips pulling upward. "Got it, boss. Any other orders?"

She bobs her head up and down with her stern face on, which is more amusing than it is anything else. "Yes, take me back to our room so I can cheer you up."

Holding onto her, I stand to my feet. "Best order ever," I say then I kiss her while carrying her to our room, grasping onto the peaceful moment with all I have in me because I have a feeling, come tomorrow, this quiet life I've been so accustomed to lately is about to turn into chaos.

SEVEN

CALLIE

I DREAM A LOT THAT NIGHT. Of Kayden. Of my past. Of the girl in the photo that Evie showed me. Of a world filled with women who feel shamed into silence. I also dream about Caleb. Normally, when he enters my dreams—or nightmares anyway—I wake up sweaty and terrified. This time, though, when my eyelids open, I'm filled with a sense of contentment. Because I know.

Know what I need to do.

Since it's his day off, Kayden is still fast asleep when I wake up, even though it's well past ten. But after the stressful night he had, I'm not surprised.

Wanting to let him rest, I grab my phone, climb out of bed, and slip into the living room. Then I sit down on the sofa and dial the number Evie gave me last night before I left.

She answers after two rings, "So?"

I smile at her directness. "I'll do it."

"I figured you would."

How she knew is beyond me since I only made up my mind a few minutes ago.

Evie spends the next few minutes giving me a few brief details. But in order to really start the job, I'll have to go down to the secret office and get the files on the victims. Easton will also be showing me the ropes and helping me while I work on this assignment. I hope Kayden is going to be okay with that since I could tell Easton bothered him. Kayden isn't controlling, though, so I don't foresee it being a problem. But I also don't want him burying his feelings away like he sometimes does. And I need to make sure that while I put almost all of my effort into this job, I'm still here for him, especially with everything going on.

Once I make plans with Evie to go down to the office later tonight, I hang up and head for the kitchen to make Kayden breakfast. I'm not much of a cook, but I can make some pretty okay scrambled eggs. As I'm cracking the eggs apart, my phone rings and *Violet* flashes across the screen. Strange. She usually texts me instead of calling.

Wiping the yoke off my fingertips, I answer the phone. "Let me guess. Seth is putting up a fuss about having to drive."

"Actually, I haven't even gotten around to calling him yet." She blows out a deafening exhale. "I know this is going to make me suck, but I can't make it today. Do you guys mind going next weekend instead? Some shit came up and there's no way in hell I can make it."

"That's fine with me. In fact, I'm sort of glad. I've got a ton of stuff going on today that I didn't know about until this morning." I grab a whisker to beat the eggs. "Is every-thing okay, though? You sound stressed out."

"I'm fine." But she sounds hoarse and upset.

"Are you sure?"

"Yep, totally cool. I promise. Luke and I just have some things to take care of today. That's all."

I'm nearly positive she's lying. But since Violet is the sort of person that won't open up to you until she's ready, I let the subject drop.

"Well, let me know if you need anything," I say. "And, if you want, I can call Seth and cancel."

"God, yes. Thank you. Thank you. Thank you. I so wasn't up for a bitch fest this morning."

"No problem."

We hang up, and I go back to cooking my eggs. I can't help but wonder what's going on with her. While Violet has been known to occasionally bail out on plans, she rarely sounds upset. Not because she never gets upset. She's just the sort of person not to show it.

"You're cooking?" Kayden wanders into the kitchen right as I'm shutting off the stove. His hair is flattened on one side, his eyes are a bit bloodshot, and he's only wearing a pair of pajama bottoms so I get a full view of his muscular chest. "Man, what's the occasion?" he teases as he comes up behind me and wraps his arms around my waist.

"Hey, I cook sometimes," I protest, playfully nudging him in the side.

He kisses the side of my head. "I know. I'm just messing with you." He nuzzles his face into the crook of my neck. "You really didn't have to cook for me, baby. I promise I'm okay."

I relax back against his chest. "I know I didn't have to, but I wanted to."

He kisses the side of my neck. "You're amazing."

My heart flutters in my chest. "You're amazing too."

We steal a few more kisses then pile the eggs onto two plates and snuggle up in bed to eat them.

A few bites in, I say, "I called Evie this morning."

He glances up from his eggs, his expression cautious. "What'd you tell her?"

"That I'd take the job." I stuff a forkful of eggs into my mouth. "I'm supposed to go down to the office today, but I should be done by the time your game starts. Maybe after that, we could go out to dinner or something. Maybe do something relaxing because I have a feeling I'm going to need it big time."

He nods, absentmindedly stirring his eggs. "That sounds good to me."

Sensing his sullen demeanor, I set my fork down, take his plate and set it aside, and then climb onto his lap. "Talk to me."

Sighing, he folds his arms around my waist. "It's nothing. My head's just stuck in a weird place."

"Is it about me taking the job?" I hesitate, not wanting to upset him more, but feel like I need to ask. "Or about this dad thing?"

"The dad thing." His shoulders heave as he exhales loudly. "I'm just not sure if I should call this guy and find out if he was telling the truth. I mean, what if he is, and it turns out I have another dad out there in the world, but he's even worse than the guy who raised me?" He swallows hard. "I don't think I can take any more shitty dads in my life."

I take a moment to choose the right words. "I think if you don't find out the truth, it's going to eat away at you. But, if it turns out this guy was telling the truth, and you do have a father out there in the world, we don't have to jump into meeting him right away." I mold the palm of my hand against his cheek. "We can look into it some more. Do some research. Find out who the guy is and then decide if he deserves to be in your life, okay?"

He nods, holding onto me tightly. "You really are perfect, you know that. And I know I'm a little nervous about this new job, but I have a feeling you're going to end up writing an amazing story."

"I sure hope so." I also hope I can handle what I'm about to do.

What I really hope is that I can do what Evie expects me to do. That I can get the story. Tell the story. Breathe the story. Feel the story.

And somehow get the victims some sort of justice.

WHILE CALLIE and I spend the morning eating breakfast in bed, I receive a message from Jason, inviting me to a party. Considering how awesome our conversation was yesterday, I'm fucking surprised by the invite. I'm also annoyed by the way he makes it a point to state that a lot of hot women are going to be there. My response?

Me: Fuck off.

Jason: Your loss, man. I was just trying to help you out.

Me: Since I don't have a problem, I don't need any help.

Jason: Keep telling yourself that.

I shake my head. This guy is seriously the most annoying person I've ever met.

"Who are you texting?" Callie wonders as she

stretches out across the bed on her stomach. "You look pissed off."

I toss the phone onto the nightstand. "This guy from my team. His name is Jason, and he thinks there's something wrong with me because I never want to go to parties."

She peers over her shoulder at me, strands of her long brown hair falling into her face. "Do you want to go to a party? Because if you do, you can. I can come too if you want me to."

I shake my head. "Now why would I want to do that?" I line my body over her's and grind my hips against her ass. When she gasps, I smile to myself. "When I could spend all night doing stuff like this." I dip my head to suck on her neck.

She whimpers, gasping my name. "That feels so good."

"It's about to feel even better." I reach for the hem of her pajama shorts, ready to pull them down so I can slip inside her.

But my damn phone rings, ruining the moment.

I debate if I should answer it. Normally, I wouldn't, but I'm expecting a call from Dylan and I—

"Answer it," Callie insists, as if sensing my confliction. "I'm not going anywhere yet."

Smiling, I give one final suck on her neck then reach

across the bed and grab my phone. When I see *Dylan* flash across the screen, I don't know whether to be relieved or terrified. Perhaps a little bit of both.

"Hey," I answer, sounding stupidly nervous.

"Hey," he replies, sounding equally as nervous. "So, I talked to Mom this morning."

"I'm guessing by your tone it didn't go well."

"Well, she was drunk off her ass and kept trying to demand that I need to come see her. So, yeah, she was basically her normal self." A beat of silence passes by then he says, "I did manage to get some information out of her, though."

"About this thing with our Dad not being my real dad?"

"Yeah."

Then he says nothing.

And the silence is fucking maddening. And makes the cut on my arm itch.

"So," I finally say. "What'd she say?"

"Is Callie with you?"

Fuck, if he's asking that, this is going to be bad.

I glance at Callie as she sits up and scoots over beside me. "Yeah, she's right here."

"Good." Another pause.

He's seriously driving me insane.

But then finally he speaks again, and I realize maybe

the silence wasn't too terrible. That maybe I should've wished for a little bit more.

"The guy was telling the truth," he says. "Mom was having an affair when she got pregnant with you, and she's almost positive Dad isn't your birth father. I asked her if he was our father too—Tyler and me—and she insisted it wasn't."

"Holy shit," I breathe out, clutching onto Callie's hand. That would mean Dylan and Tyler are only my half-brothers. "Did Dad know about this?"

"I'm not sure." Uncertainty rings in his tone, making me wonder if he's having the same thoughts as me.

That perhaps Dad did know and that's why he gave me the most severe beatings, going as far as stabbing me.

The scar on my side burns as I remember when he pushed the knife into me.

"Kayden, are you still there?" Dylan asks worriedly.

I nod, even though he can't see me. "Yeah, I'm still here... I was just wondering about some stuff."

"Do you want me to fly out there? Just say the word, and I can be there in a day."

"Maybe." A drop of ease rushes through me as Callie skims her finger along the inside of my wrist. "Let me talk to Callie, and I'll let you know."

"Okay." Worry crams his tone. "Call me later, okay? Liz and I worry about you."

"I know." I suck in a breath. "Thanks for doing this... and for worrying about me."

"You're my brother, Kayden. Of course I worry."

We say goodbye and then I hang up.

Callie doesn't ask what happened. She simply loops her arms around me and hugs me tightly.

"We're going to get through this," she promises. "You and I, we can beat anything."

I slide my arms around her waist and hug her back. "I know."

And I mean it. There's nothing Callie and I can't overcome. Still, it doesn't mean I'm not fucking terrified or that deep down, part of me craves the graze of a razor blade. But I crave her hugs more, so I hold on tight and let her hold me up from sinking.

Silence builds around us. I know she's waiting for me to speak first.

"The guy was telling the truth," I whisper. "My dad probably isn't my birth father."

She nods, probably already putting that together based on my reaction. "What do you want to do?"

"I think I need to call this private eye guy and get the name of this guy who says he's my birth father. Then do some research on him. And if I decide to meet him, I'm probably going to have to get a DNA test done because my mom wasn't one hundred percent sure." I clutch onto her even more tightly. "I'm sorry. This is probably the last thing you need to be dealing with right after you got hired for this new job."

"You're more important than some job—you're more important than anything." She pulls back to meet my gaze. "I want to be here for you while you go through this. No keeping me out of the loop because you think it'll be better for me, okay?"

I nod. "But only if you do the same for me with this job. No keeping me in the dark because you're afraid I'll worry about you."

"It's a deal." She sticks out her pinkie. "Now pinkie swear on it."

I hitch my pinkie through hers. Then I press my lips to hers, deciding a kiss is a way better method of sealing a promise. In that moment, even with the chaos swirling around me, everything feels calm. That's what Callie does for me. She helps me survive the chaos. And it's probably a good thing too since I have a feeling the chaos is just starting.

NINE
CALLIE

AFTER KAYDEN and I eat breakfast, I start getting ready for the day. While I'm digging through the closet for an outfit, my phone rings with an incoming call from my mom. Since I'm pressed for time, I almost ignore it. But she has been trying to get a hold of me for the last few days, so…

Sighing, I answer the phone. "Hey, Mom."

"Hey, honey!" Her cheerfulness isn't out of the ordinary, but the banging noises in the background are.

"What's going on over there?" I sink down onto the bed. "It sounds noisy."

"We're working on the bedroom above the garage for when you guys come out here this summer."

"Um, yeah, I'm not sure if we're going to be able to make it or not. There's a lot of stuff going on, and I got this new job, and I'm not sure what the hours are going to be like yet."

"You got a new job?" She doesn't sound as thrilled as I had hoped.

"You act like that's a bad thing?"

"No, it's not. It's great. It's just...." She trails off, but I know she isn't finished.

I let a slow exhale ease from my lips, preparing myself for whatever she's about to say. Even after I told my parents about what happened with Caleb, my mom and I still don't always get along or see eye to eye.

"What about getting married?" she finally asks. "Have you thought any more about that?"

"I already told you we're not. We're still young. And I know it bothers you that we're living together, but it's not as weird as you think it is." With a quick glance at the time, I put the phone on speaker, set it on the dresser, and then return to the closet to search for an outfit.

"Still... you guys are close enough that you should at least talk about it," she tells me.

I internally sigh. We've had this conversation before, many, many times, and it's pointless to argue with her. "We do," I lie.

We don't. Not because I don't think about forever with Kayden, but because like I told my mom, we're still young.

My mom and I chat for a few more minutes before I tell her I have to go. As I'm hanging up, a message pings through from Seth.

Seth: Have you talked to Violet recently?

Me: She called me earlier to say she had to cancel on our plans today. I was actually about to text you about it. Why? What's up?

Seth: She called me to ask if she could borrow my car for a little bit this morning, which is weird. And she was acting strange. I think she had been crying.

Worry seeps through me. Violet rarely cries, at least in front of people.

Me: I thought she was acting a bit weird too. Did she say why?

Seth: No. But you know how she is. I think we should stop by and check on her.

Me: How about we pick her up for the game?

Seth: Sounds good to me. I'll text her.

Me: Okay. TTYL. And let me know if you find out what's going on.

Seth: Will do.

I'm about to put the phone down when another message comes through.

Seth: Wait, hold on. So, we're really not going shopping today then?

Me: Yeah, sorry. Violet said she had to cancel and I'm kind of busy too.

Seth: Well, we need to reschedule then and soon. I want to look amazing for summer break. And FYI, you guys owe me a coffee for standing me up!

Me: We figured as much already.

I set the phone down with an unsettling feeling stirring inside me. Violet's life hasn't been easy. She's been through a lot—more than most people.

"I hope everything's okay with her," I mutter, combing my fingers through my hair.

Then, because I know I have to focus right now, I take a deep breath, set the worry aside, and focus on getting ready for my new job. I'm not going to lie and say I'm not terrified—I am. But I'm also excited for this new adventure in my life. I just hope I can balance my job and my personal life. And that I can be here for Kayden. But with Kayden by my side, I feel like can handle just about anything.

I hope...

TEN
KAYDEN

EVAN MERILIIEFORD IS the name listed on the detective agency card. The address and phone number is in Laramie, which means the man who believes he's my father lives in Laramie, or he knows I live here and hired a detective from the same town I reside in.

As I sit on the sofa in my apartment, patting the card against the palm of my hand, I try to decide the best time to call this guy. Honestly, I'm not sure there is a "best time" when it comes to calling up a person who could potentially tell you all the Hell you suffered through for your entire life could've been avoided. I mean, what happens if the man that hired this Evan detective guy is my birth father and he turns out to be a great guy, way better than the monster I believed was my dad for almost my entire life? What if he would've taken me in had he known about me when I was born. What if I could've grown up not being tortured, beaten, and loathed.

What if…

What if…

What if…

Yeah, I really need to stop going down this road before I end up sinking into a pit of depression.

The moment Callie leaves the house for her new job, I start to obsess over the card until I glance at the time and realize I need to be down at the stadium in less than a few hours. Since I have a game tonight, it might be best if I stop worrying about this for now and call the number tomorrow. Sure, my head will be crammed with a ton of worry, but trying to deal with this only hours before a game is going to pull me out of the state of mind I have to be in when I step out on the field. A state of mind that has no room for worries of fathers and lives that never happened.

Pushing to my feet, I grab my wallet and tuck the card inside the flap. Then I head back to the bedroom to take a quick nap before the game starts since I spent half the night tossing and turning over this whole father thing.

Right as I'm about to lie down, my phone rings from inside my pocket. Sighing, I fish it out, noting the call is from Luke.

"Hey, man," I say as I flop down on the bed.

"Hey." He pauses for a lengthy amount of time. "Look, so this is going to sound a bit strange, and you're probably going to have a lot of questions, but I can't answer them right now."

"Um... Okay." What the hell? "Is everything okay?"

"Yeah, kind of." He pauses again. "I just wanted to give you a heads up that I quit the team."

"What?" I sit up, startled and confused as fuck. "When?"

"A couple of hours ago." A loud breath puffs through the line. "It's not a big deal. It's not like I was ever going to get drafted or anything. Football was just something I did for fun and to keep myself busy, but some stuff came up and... Well, yeah, I gotta quit the team."

"What kind of stuff came up?"

"Well, see here's the thing. I actually can't answer that. I want to, man. My life would be way fucking easier if I could. But I literally can't. And I'm begging you not to push this because it's pointless and I'll just have to keep saying the same thing over and over again."

"Everything's okay, though, right?"

"Kind of. I mean, with the reason I have to quit." He sighs. "Violet's not taking this don't-ask-questions thing very well, though. "

"You didn't tell her either?" I'm unable to conceal my shock.

"Not because I don't want to. Because I can't." He huffs out a breath. "She's so fucking pissed off. She even borrowed Seth's car, packed her shit, and is telling me she's going to stay in a hotel." He sounds on the verge of panicking. "So, if you have any advice on how to smooth this over, please tell me because I'm seriously lost."

"My advice is to tell her what the hell is going on." I rake my fingers through my hair. "Maybe you do have a good reason for not telling me or anyone else why you quit the team, but she's your girlfriend, and you need to make an exception with her."

"What if I legally can't?"

Huh? "Okay, now you're really confusing the fuck out of me."

"I know." He sighs again. "I'll figure something out. I just wanted to give you a heads up that I'm not going to be at the game today. And that you might be seeing less of me for the next couple of months."

"You know, you sound sketchy as shit now, right?"

"Yep, I sure do."

"Cool, just as long as you know that."

"Always do." He blows out a breath. "I gotta go. I've got this... thing later today that I have to get ready for."

I reach for a glass of water that's on the nightstand and take a sip. "Well, if you need anything, just let me know."

"I will." He hesitates. "Everything going well with

you, though? I know we haven't gotten to hang out much lately."

"I honestly don't know how to answer that question." I set the glass of water down. "There's some crazy shit that's going on right now... With my dad."

"With your *dad*?"

"Yeah... Look, it's a complicated story that I don't really feel like talking about yet—not until I find out a few things. But how about we plan on hanging out next weekend or something. You and Violet can come over here, and we can grill some burgers. I know Callie's been wanting to do that. We can invite Seth and Greyson too."

"Let me double check on something and I'll let you know," he says hesitantly. "I might have some... other stuff going on next weekend."

"You're not joining the mob or anything like that, are you?" I joke. Well, partially joke.

I've been best friends with Luke for a long fucking time and know he's gotten into some trouble over the years —we both have. But Luke almost seems to crave trouble sometimes and even goes looking for it.

"Nah, this is nothing like that," he assures me. "What's going on... It's good for me. It's just going to complicate my personal life for a bit. But I promise, eventually, I'll be able to tell you more."

"All right. Well, let me know if you need anything.

And let me know about next weekend."

"Will do."

We hang up, and I roll over to go to sleep when the doorbell rings.

"Son of a bitch," I grumble as I bury my head further into the pillows.

I'm not answering the damn door. I'm going to get some rest. I can't take any more drama right now. Whoever they are will go away—

The bell rings again, this time twice in a row. It's followed by a loud knock.

I shake my head before dragging my ass out of bed. Kicking some clothes out of the way, I walk out of the room, across the living room, and throw open the doorway.

My eyes instantly narrow, my jaw ticking, my fingers curling into fists. "What the fuck are you doing here."

My mother smiles at me, but her eyes are filled with the emotional coldness I grew up despising. "You and I need to talk."

She looks just like she used to, her hair perfectly in place, not a wrinkle in her designer dress, and a string of pearls is around her neck. She always loved giving off the appearance that her life was all flashy perfection and smiles. But if someone looks close enough, they'll see her bloodshot eyes, which are due to the fact that she constantly drinks and pops pills. And behind that plastic smile is a dark and haunting coldness she rarely shows anyone except her family.

Lucky us.

"Fuck off." I move to shut the door in her face.

"You can't talk to him," she sputters in desperation.

I've never heard her sound so desperate and maybe that's why I pause.

"Talk to who?" I ask with the door half closed.

Her gaze flicks to the stairwell and then to the parking lot before she looks back at me. "Your father."

"Which one, Mother?" I crook a brow. "The man I grew up believing was my father. You know, the one that you let beat me for years. Because he's buried about six feet under the ground right now and I'm thinking it's pretty impossible to talk to him." I slant against the door-frame and stare her down as she glares at me. "Or the man I just found out about last night. You know, the man you apparently had an affair with and who I never knew existed until about twenty-four hours ago when some stranger came up and informed me. Thanks for that, by the way. For not telling me."

Her lip twitches. "You've grown bolder since the last time I spoke to you."

"Yeah, because I realized I didn't have to take your shit anymore."

"Just because you decided I wasn't good enough to be in your life anymore, doesn't give you the right to talk to me this way."

"I'm not saying anything that isn't true," I clarify. "And I told you a long time ago that I didn't want you in my life anymore. That you're toxic. So when you show up at my front door unannounced, this is the sort of treatment you're going to get, especially after I just found out you've been lying to me for my entire life."

"I didn't lie to you," she hisses, stepping forward to get into my face. "I was protecting you."

"Protecting me?" I gape at her. "Protecting me from what? The fact that the man I grew up thinking was my father might not be. That all those years of torture and mental mind fucks could have never happened."

Her eyes narrow to slits. "You think just because some man claims he's your father that he's going to be better than the man that raised you." She inches toward me, her eyes full of a rage I've never been able to understand. "A bit of advice, Kayden. The man who's about to try to barge into your life is nothing but a coldhearted monster. You can let him in if you want, but you'll regret it eventually, just like I did." Her voice cracks, and for a moment her eyes reflect so much emotion that I barely recognize her. But just as swiftly as it appears, the emotion fizzles into that familiar emptiness. Smoothing her hands over her hair, she steps back. "Now, when you're ready to talk, you can give me a call." She hands me a card. "I'm staying in a hotel downtown. I'll be here in Laramie for about a week while I take care of some things. Then I'm returning home."

She doesn't mention where home is and I don't bother asking. She just turns away and hurries down the stairway while I step back and slam the door.

I glance at the card she gave me, note her phone number scribbled on the back, and crumble it up.

Like hell I'm ever going to purposefully contact that woman again.

And how the hell did she track me down so fast? Or has she been living near Laramie this entire time and I was just unaware?

"Fuck." I slam my hand against the door, anger and tension rippling through me.

So much for relaxing before the game.

I can't believe this is happening. Can't believe she's affecting me like this again. I shouldn't let her fuck with my head, but I can't help but worry about what she said. That maybe this man who might be my real birth father is worse than the man I grew up believing was my father.

But can I just take her word for it?

Fuck no. My mom's one of the biggest liars I know.

But what if she's telling the truth this time?

I'LL ADMIT, I'm nervous as I make my way to the bookshop. The sign on the front door is flipped to *closed* and the door is locked. Like Evie instructed last night, I dig my key out of my pocket and unlock the door. For some reason, I cast a glance around the quiet area before slipping inside and locking the door back up again.

The lights are off inside, but the sunlight from outside filters in through the small windows and lights a path down the row of bookshelves to the far back door with all the deadbolts. I unlock all of those with the same key I used on the front door then I twist the knob and just like that, I'm starting my very first day of my new job.

The space hidden behind the door is far less busy than it was last night; only one other person is there, typing away at a computer. I look around, searching for

Evie and spot her in the back office we went into last night. She notices me at almost the same time and motions me over.

I smile then make my way around the cluttered computer desks and to her office.

"Callie, glad you made it through the doors." She shoves a stack of papers aside. "Sadly, not everyone does. I haven't figured out yet if it's because they're nervous and decide to back out, or if the locks are too complicated for them. If it's the latter, I'm glad they never made it back here."

I lower my bag to the floor and sink into a chair. "I kind of understand the nervous part," I admit, wiping my damp palms on the front of my jeans. "I feel like I'm bursting with energy right now."

"That's a good thing. It means you're excited." She smiles at me before taking a sip from a coffee mug.

"I am," I say. "I just hope I can do a good job. And maybe get those girls some justice."

"You wouldn't be here if I didn't think you could." She pulls open the top desk drawer. "All right, let's get straight to the point since you've got a lot of work cut out for you." She drops a small stack of folders in front of me. "Each folder contains information about a victim and the details of their attack. I'd like you to spend the weekend going over this information. I'm going to give you Easton's phone number before you leave here. If you have any questions about the files, call him or call me. And I mean that, Callie. Day or night, you can call me or Easton, even if it's to have a mini meltdown." She rests her arms on the desk. "This job is going to be extremely stressful and time-consuming, and I don't want you thinking you're in it alone. If you think this way, then you probably won't make it past day one."

I nod. "I promise I'll call if I need anything."

"Good." She mulls something over. "Easton mentioned when he stopped by your apartment the other night to give you the welcome gift that your boyfriend answered the door."

I nod, unsure what this has to do with anything. "Yeah, we live together."

She nods contemplatively. "Have you talked to him about this job at all?"

"I told him a little bit about the job." Okay, that's a lie. And while I'm not typically a liar, I signed a non-disclosure agreement. "Not the specifics, though."

"But he understands you'll be working long hours?" she asks, and I nod. "He's supportive then?"

I nod again. "Kayden's a great guy, which is part of the reason I love him so much." There are so many other reasons, though, but she doesn't need to hear about all of them.

"Good." Her serious expression fades into a smile. "Sorry, I had to go there. I just want to make sure there won't be any hiccups in the future when we start putting you on bigger stories that require a lot of travel time and maybe even relocation."

I keep on smiling, but inside my heart drops. Bigger stories? Traveling? Relocation? Why hadn't I thought about that before? Maybe because I've never liked my other jobs enough to envision a future at the companies? I wonder if I'll like this job enough to want to stay. So far, I can see the potential.

What if I do? Then what will happen with Kayden and me?

ABOUT AN HOUR LATER, I leave the secret office—not sure how much of a secret it is, but that's what I'm calling it for now—with a stack of folders in my arms that contain the victims' information, along with Easton's number and a bunch of other contacts. After I pile the files onto the passenger seat of my car, I climb into the driver's side with the intention of driving home before I start delving into the folders. But curiosity gets the best of me and I peek inside the top folder before even starting up the engine.

The moment I see the first name on the paper, my heart clenches. Harper Allyberriton, who's my age, attends UW, and who was once my roommate before I moved in with Kayden. She had come to me once and told me about the time she was raped, figuring I could relate to her. She was fourteen when the rape happened, and while she never flat out said it, I wondered if perhaps the person who raped her was her stepfather. I didn't know her well enough to be certain, though, and moved out of the dorms not long after she confided in me. Since Harper and I don't have any classes together and no mutual friends we sort of drifted apart. Still, my chest aches reading that she was raped again and recently.

"How is this life?" I whisper to myself as I pick up the paper that contains the details of her attack, which is a whole whopping three lines and doesn't list the name of the attacker, only that she was at a party and that she remembers something about the term The LW Shadow Circle being thrown around. I have no clue what this circle thing is or how it's connected to the attack. I wish there was more information, but Evie had warned me that these girls were either scared or being blackmailed into silence. Maybe if I could get them to open up to me and tell me more information, it would help. Then again, Evie did mention some of the girls were drugged, so they might only remember the details listed on these papers.

I swallow the lump forming in my throat as memories of the day I was raped prickle in my mind. I was very much aware of what happened, the images vivid and nauseating.

"Suck it up, Callie," I tell myself. "You can do this."

When I turn the page, though, and see the photo taken of Harper right after the incident occurred, her face swollen, her lip cut, her bloodshot eyes hollow, vomit works its way up my throat. Shoving the door open, I puke out the eggs I ate for breakfast all over the asphalt.

Taking a shaky inhale, I wipe my mouth off with my sleeve, straighten, and shut the door. Throwing up isn't a great start, but I don't want to let that discourage me.

My gaze drifts to the file of Harper. No, I refuse to let it discourage me. I'll figure out a way to get these girls justice, no matter what it takes.

BY THE TIME I arrive home, I barely have any time before I have to head down to the stadium to watch Kayden's game. I'm just about to get changed into something more comfortable before I take off when my phone rings. Figuring its Kayden, since he usually calls me around this time, I answer my phone without checking the screen.

"Callie?" The voice that greets me when I answer isn't Kayden.

"Um, yeah, this is her," I reply, confused at first but then recognition clicks.

Easton.

"Hey," he says. "I just wanted to check in and see how things were going. Evie said you picked up the files for project Injustice today?"

"Project Injustice?"

"Yeah, we give all of our stories nicknames, and with yours, Injustice just seemed fitting."

"Oh. Yeah, sorry I got confused." I open up the top dresser drawer and dig out a pair of my favorite jeans. "Evie never mentioned the name."

"Yeah, she sometimes tends to forget the smaller details. She's a great boss and a great journalist, but she usually takes on too much and can get sort of scatter-brained. But that's what I'm there for. Well, that and to make sure the newbies don't lose their minds on their first job," he teases. "Which is sort of why I was calling. To make sure you're doing okay after reading the files."

"I'm fine." I balance the phone between my shoulder and ear as I undo the zipper and button of the pants I'm wearing. "I haven't gotten through all the folders yet, but I will tonight."

"Take your time," he says. "You should probably even read through them a couple of times."

"I was planning on it." I slip my pants off and kick them aside. "I actually knew one of the girls. She was my roommate for a little while during the beginning of the year before I moved out of the dorms."

"Really?" he asks, intrigued. "Which one was it?"

"Harper Allyberriton." I pull on the pair of jeans I grabbed from the dresser. "I don't know her very well, but

I do have some information on her that's not listed in the folder. I need to talk to her first before I add the information, though, and make sure she's okay with it."

"That's good. That you know her, I mean. She might be more willing to open up to you."

"I hope so. I'll probably call her tomorrow and see if she wants to meet up for coffee or something."

"That's a good start. If you need any help with anything, give me a shout."

"Thanks. I definitely will." I grab a black T-shirt from the dresser, hurry and put the phone on speaker, and set it down on the bed. "Can I ask you a question?"

"Sure."

I tug the shirt I'm wearing off. "How long have you been working for Evie?"

He counts under his breath. "Since I was a sophomore, so about three years."

"Do you, or did you, go to UW?" I ask, pulling the clean shirt over my head.

"I did go there," he replies. "I graduated last year but continued working for *The Offbeat Go Daily* because I love the job. It's hard to find a writing job with so much freedom."

"I completely understand that. It's part of the reason why I was looking for a new job to begin with." I wander into the bathroom to get a brush. "So you've never had to relocate or go on long trips for your job? Because Evie mentioned today that I might have to do both."

"I've had to do a lot of traveling and relocation has been mentioned a few times, but since I'm Evie's assistant on top of being a journalist, she's yet to really push me into moving to a different office. I think she likes having me around too much," he says in a light tone "Although, she'll probably never admit that."

I frown. Crap. That wasn't the answer I was hoping for.

"A lot of her other journalists have relocated though, to bigger cities, which means better stories," he adds. "That's probably something to keep in mind as you move forward with this job."

"I will." I aim for an upbeat tone, but inside I feel deflated.

I really need to talk to Kayden about this, so we can come up with a plan if that happens down the road. I just hope we can come up with something that doesn't require us being apart from each other for long periods of time. Or that requires one of us to give up our dreams.

NORMALLY, I drive to the games with Seth, Greyson, and Violet, but apparently, Luke quit the team. I'm unsure why—Violet was extremely vague in her text. And Seth and Greyson are going to be a little bit late, so I decide to drive by myself today.

Since I'm a little bit early, the parking lot isn't too crowded when I pull up. After parking my car, I make my way to the stadium while sending Kayden a text.

Me: Hey, just made it here. Good luck today!

He usually doesn't respond for at least a couple of minutes whenever a game's about to start, so his almost immediate response startles me.

Kayden: Glad you texted. Can you meet me at the entrance before you head in? There's

something I need to get off my chest before the game starts.

With everything going on in his life right now, worry stirs inside me that perhaps something else—maybe something bad—has happened.

Me: Headed there right now.

I rush toward the entrance and find him waiting for me in front of one of the gates. He's dressed in his uniform sans his helmet and his brown hair is a tousled mess. He's frowning as I approach, but when his gaze finds mine a relieved smile breaks across his face.

"Hey," I start, but he silences me with a deep, intense kiss that tingles across my entire body and leaves me breathless.

"Hey." He brushes his mouth across mine again, slowly, as if savoring the feel of my lips.

I stand on my tiptoes and loop my arms around the back of his neck. "Is everything okay?"

He nods, resting his forehead against mine. "Now that you're here, it is."

I trace a path up and down the nape of his neck. "What happened? Because I can tell something did."

He sighs, his lean arms winding around my waist. "My mom showed up at our place today."

I jerk my head back to look at him, unsure if he's

joking or not. By the serious expression on his face, I can tell he's not.

"Seriously?" I ask, and he nods. "Why? And how does she even know where we live?"

"I never got around to asking her how she found our address, although she could've easily looked it up or asked around." His hold on me tightens. "As for the why…" He shakes his head, the muscle in his jaw spasming. "She said she wanted to warn me about this man claiming to be my biological father." His throat muscles work as he swallows hard. "She said he's bad. Even worse than the bastard I grew up thinking was my father."

I move my hand to cup his cheek. "Do you think she was telling the truth?"

He leans into my touch. "It's hard to say with her." He releases an uneven exhale. "She had the audacity to say she was going to be in town for the next week and that I should come see her." He shakes his head. "Like I want to put myself through that torture."

"Then don't go see her." I give him a soft kiss on the lips. "We don't need her for this. We can talk to the detective on our own, get the name of this man that claims he's your biological father, and then do some research on him. And if we need any outside help, we can go to Dylan."

He hugs me closer. "Thank you for saying that. I think deep down I already knew that, but for some reason I needed to hear it from someone else... Needed to be reminded that I have other people in my life and I don't have to rely on my mom anymore."

"That's what I'm here for." I easily give in as he pulls me in for a kiss, our tongues tangling, our bodies perfectly aligned.

We kiss for a couple more minutes before he heads back to the locker room.

As I make my way to the stands, my mind gets stuck on Kayden and ways I can make him realize everything will be okay, no matter how this all turns out. But I get torn from Kayden Worry Land as I'm rounding the corner and catch the faint sounds of a heated conversation coming from the women's bathroom. I'm not one to intervene in other people's business, but a loud bang makes me pause and then move toward the door.

"You tell anyone about happened the other night and I'll end you," a deep, male voice whispers. "Do you understand?"

"Yes," a woman sobs. "I didn't mean for anyone to find out."

"This is your last chance, Maddie," the guy warns. "Any more slip-ups and you're done with."

Footsteps stomp across the floor, growing louder. I skitter out of the way and around the corner as the door swings open. As the air grows quiet, I suck in a breath and peek around the corner. A tall figure, dressed head to toe in black with the hood of his jacket pulled over his head is striding away from the women's bathroom. His back is to me so I can't see his face, but I still take out my phone and snap a photo of him. Then I hurry into the bathroom to check on the woman he was threatening.

Soft crying flows through the air as I step inside.

"Hello?" I call out as I walk past the stalls.

The soft crying falters.

"I just wanted to see if you were okay," I explain as I reach the stall I'm pretty sure she's in.

"I heard yelling and crying and..." *And what, Callie? You don't even know what's going on.*

"I'm fine," the woman whispers back hoarsely. "And even if I wasn't, I couldn't talk to you about it. If they found out I told you—told you what they did to me..." Her voice cracks. "They'd destroy me."

"What if I promised not to tell anyone?" I offer. "Would that help?"

She laughs hollowly. "They'd find out. They always do." The door swings open. Standing on the other side is a woman around my age with long, blonde hair and blood-shot eyes. Mascara is running down her cheeks, and the strap of her dress is torn. "Do yourself a favor," she bites out bitterly. "Stay away from The LW Shadow Circle."

"LW Shadow Circle?" My mind races as I recall what I read in Harper's file. "What is that exactly?"

She doesn't answer, pushing past me and hurrying for the door. It takes me a moment to unglue my feet from the floor and chase after her. But by the time I make it out of the bathroom, she's long gone.

I rake my fingers through my hair, my mind running a million miles a minute. The LW Shadow Circle was briefly mentioned in Harper's file but was never explained.

Pulling out my phone, I type the name into the search engine but get no useful results. I make a note in my phone to talk to Easton about it, then add the description of the woman I talked to in the bathroom. The guy called her Maddie but never used her last name. If she attends UW, though, I may be able to track her down and see if I can persuade her into talking to me some more about this LW Shadow Circle and about whatever they did to her.

While I'm not sure, I have to wonder if this Maddie girl may be an unreported victim.

As people begin to pour into the stadium, I put my phone away and make my way toward the section my seat is located in. When I sit down, I work on getting myself into the right mindset to cheer Kayden on. Usually, I can do so without a lot of complications, but my mind is all over the place right now. Maddie seemed so scared and worried, but what was she so afraid of? This LW Shadow Circle? Is it a frat perhaps? A club? A club for what, though?

Or maybe it could be a secret society, but that seems like a stretch. I mean, I know they exist and everything, but in Laramie?

I massage my temples as I feel a headache approaching. Between that and throwing up earlier, I'm not feeling so great. If I'm going to make this new job work, I'll have to find a way to handle my stress better. Maybe hit the gym more. Do more kickboxing exercises. Maybe eat more too since my stomach is grumbling like a crazy Gremlin right now.

I start to get up to hit the concession stand when I receive a phone call from Violet.

"Hey," I answer as I make my way down the aisle toward the stairway. "I'm glad you called. Seth keeps bugging me about rescheduling our shopping trip. Any ideas of when you'll be down so I can tell him and hopefully get him to shush for a bit?"

"Well, I'd love to set a time and date, but I need a favor first." She sounds exhausted. "Can you come down to the police station and pick my sorry ass up?"

I screech to a halt, nearly tripping over my feet. "You're at the police station?"

"Yeah, I got arrested earlier, but then got released. But

this detective dude friend of mine, who helped me get released, won't let me leave the station unless I have someone come pick me up because he thinks I'm unstable." She raises her voice, her tone oozing with irritation. "Coming from the guy that just broke a coffee mug because I was testing his patience."

Somebody curses in the background and Violet snickers.

"But yeah, anyway," she says to me. "I'd really appreciate it if you'd come pick me up. I know you're at a game and everything, but I tried to call Greyson and he won't answer his phone. And Seth will drill me with too many questions if I ask him."

"Yeah, he definitely would." I pause. "What about Luke, though?"

"I'm not talking to him right now." Her tone is emotionless, which in Violet language means she's hurting about something and doesn't want to talk about it.

Knowing not to press her, I hurry down the stairs. "All right, I'm on my way. See you in about thirty minutes."

When I get off the phone with her, I'll need to send Kayden a message and let him know what's going on. I hate the idea of missing a game, especially with all the craziness going on right now, but I can't just leave Violet at the police station. Hopefully, Kayden won't be too upset. I doubt it, but I still feel bad.

"Awesome," Violet says with relief. "Thanks. I owe you one."

"No worries." I weave around the people in my way. "Although, I hope you're not in too much trouble."

"As much trouble as I'm ever in." She laughs, but the sound is all sorts of wrong, more haunted than humorous.

An idea hits me then as I'm reminded of Violet's shaky past and how she used to hang around with some sketchy people.

"Can I ask you a quick question?" I say as I reach the bottom of the stairway.

"Sure. It'll keep me from having to do small talk with Detective Smiley Face Tie."

Not sure what that's about, but I can ask her later.

"Have you ever heard of a thing called The LW Shadow Circle?" I ask as I squeeze through crowds of people.

A beat of silence ticks by and then she whispers, "Are you out in the open right now? Around other people?"

The worry in her tone causes me to freeze, my gaze skimming around the mobs of people surrounding me. "Um, yeah, I'm at the stadium... Why?"

"Do yourself a favor and keep that question and that name to yourself until you're alone," she replies lowly. "If the wrong person overhears you talking about it, you'll be in deep shit. Seriously, that's a dangerous term to throw around."

I want to ask her why. I want to ask her who I'll be in deep shit with. I want to ask her a lot of things, but I instead listen to her warning and keep my lips zipped as I hurry for my car.

I'll keep quiet for now. But if this group does have something to do with these girls' attacks, I'm going to have to speak out, no matter how dangerous they are.

ABOUT THE AUTHOR

About the Author

Jessica Sorensen is a *New York Times* and *USA Today* bestselling author who lives in the snowy mountains of Wyoming. When she's not writing, she spends her time reading and hanging out with her family.

ALSO BY JESSICA SORENSEN

Other books by Jessica Sorensen:

The Coincidence Mysteries:

The Coincidence Mysteries: The Evermore

The Coincidence Mysteries: The Invitation (coming soon)

The Coincidence Series:

The Coincidence of Callie and Kayden

The Redemption of Callie and Kayden

The Destiny of Violet and Luke

The Probability of Violet and Luke

The Certainty of Violet and Luke

The Resolution of Callie and Kayden

Seth & Greyson

Shadow Cove Series:

What Lies in the Darkness

What Lies in the Dark

Untitled (coming soon)

<u>Tangled Realms:</u>

Forever Violet

Untitled (Legend's story) (coming soon)

<u>Unexpected Series:</u>

The Unexpected

The Unpredictable

Untitled (coming soon)

<u>Curse of the Vampire Queen:</u>

Tempting Raven

Enchanting Raven

Untitled (coming soon)

<u>Mystic Willow Bay Witches Series:</u>

The Secret Life of a Witch

Broken Magic

Untitled (coming soon)

<u>Standalones:</u>

The Forgotten Girl

<u>Honeyton:</u>

The Illusion of Annabella

Sins & Secrets:

Seduction & Temptation

Sins & Secrets

Untitled (coming soon)

Rebels & Misfits:

Confessions of a Kleptomaniac

Rules of a Rebel and a Shy Girl

The Heartbreaker Society:

The Opposite of Ordinary

Broken City Series:

Nameless

Forsaken

Oblivion

Forbidden (coming soon)

Guardian Academy Series:

Entranced

Entangled

Enchanted

Entice (coming soon)

<u>**Sunnyvale Series:**</u>

The Year I Became Isabella Anders

The Year of Falling in Love

The Year of Second Chances

<u>**Unraveling You Series:**</u>

Unraveling You

Raveling You

Awakening You

Inspiring You

Fated by Darkness

Untitled (coming soon)

<u>**The Secret Series:**</u>

The Prelude of Ella and Micha

The Secret of Ella and Micha

The Forever of Ella and Micha

The Temptation of Lila and Ethan

The Ever After of Ella and Micha

Lila and Ethan: Forever and Always

Ella and Micha: Infinitely and Always

<u>**The Shattered Promises Series:**</u>

Shattered Promises

Fractured Souls

Unbroken

Broken Visions

Scattered Ashes

Breaking Nova Series:

Breaking Nova

Saving Quinton

Delilah: The Making of Red

Nova and Quinton: No Regrets

Tristan: Finding Hope

Wreck Me

Ruin Me

The Fallen Star Series:

The Fallen Star

The Underworld

The Vision

The Promise

The Lost Soul

The Evanescence

The Darkness Falls Series:

Darkness Falls

Darkness Breaks

Darkness Fades

The Death Collectors Series (NA and YA):

Ember X and Ember

Cinder X and Cinder

Spark X and Spark

Unbeautiful Series:

Unbeautiful

Untamed

Lexi Ashford:

Diary of Lexi Ashford

Untitled (coming soon)

Ultraviolet:

Ultraviolet

Untitled (coming soon)